Dragon Tales & Stories

DREW HENRIKSEN

Dragon Tales & Stories

Book Two

The Dragon and the Detective

By

DREW HENRIKSEN

Dragon Tales & Stories
Book Two

The Dragon and the Detective

A Novel By

Drew Henriksen

ISBN: 1-59507-106-7

Published by
ArcheBooks Publishing Incorporated

www.archebooks.com

9101 W. Sahara Ave., Suite 105-112
Las Vegas, NV 89117

Illustrations by Rob Granito
All illustrations used by permission.

First Edition: 2006

ArcheBooks Publishing

Dedication

Holly, Karl, Nora and Rich

And a Special Thanks to Tom Crean
for his expertise

Chapter 1

THE DETECTIVE

"How could this happen?" Frank asked Petey. "That little shit fucked with me for the last time!"

The boss was mad. Petey had *never* seen him like this. It made him very nervous. When people like the boss got pissed, they became very stupid—and very mean.

Keeping his eyes on the road, Petey tried to defuse the situation before it escalated. "Boss, he's a cop. You can't touch him. Give it time, it will blow over."

"Fuck that noise!" Frank shouted, crushing his cigar in his hand. "That shithead is getting people to notice us."

Petey thought that notion was funny, ironic really, since they were driving a stretch limo. Wisely, he kept that fact to himself. Now that he'd been promoted to Frank's driver, he watched every word, every syllable that came out of his mouth. With the shit just beginning to hit the fan, he wished he had been passed over.

"I'm going to get that worm! I'm going to get him, *and* his family," Frank growled.

Petey didn't like hearing this. Just knowing the boss wanted to go after this guy's family made him an accessory. Offing straight cops and their kids was not his thing. Offing jamokes in the business was okay; they knew what they were getting into.

"Boss, listen to yourself. It's not smart." *There, I said it*, Petey thought. *Maybe I shouldn't have.*

Petey realized he shouldn't have immediately. He got the worst of all responses, silence. It seemed like a half an hour before Frank spoke. The dreaded diamond pinky ring started tapping on the window.

"You think I'm stupid?" Frank asked.

"No boss, I said it wasn't smart to go after a cop. Especially one like this." Petey tried to explain without showing his growing fear.

"And what am I supposed to do, Professor Dumbo? Let people see this shit walk all over me?" Frank dictated more than asked.

"He's baiting you, boss. What he has on you is nothing big." Petey's voice cracked.

"You know, Petey, you're right. Instead of showing who's top dog around here, I'll let everyone see me with my dick limp! I used to like you, Petey."

Oh shit!! This isn't good!

"Pull up to Oscar's. I need more cigars," Frank said softly.

If I'm lucky, he'll just get another driver.

Oscar's was one of a few cigar shops that could get cigars from Havana. The parking lot itself was small, a bitch to pull into, and the angle sucked. To get the long limo in Petey had to make the turn from two lanes over. The last thing he wanted to do at that moment was to pull in and out fifteen times. Luckily, it was late at night and the traffic was nothing. Something had actually gone right and Petey was able to pull the limo in with ease.

"Go in and get me two boxes, and I don't want to hear your fucking mouth the rest of the night. *Capish?*" Frank announced.

Petey nodded his head, got out, and disappeared into the small shop. Frank Gercio stewed in his leather seat. As soon as he got back to the house, he decided, he was going to get rid this dumbass driver. Nobody seemed to have any balls any more, except his daughter. The one person Frank Gercio was actually worried about was his only child. Stupid ass cops did not phase him in the least. But how did that dick, Scalici, know to bust the market at that exact time? Maybe pussy boy in the shop had been talkin'. Nobody messed with him or his business, *nobody*. The cop lived on Long Island and had a daughter. Frank decided he was going to show this cop what it was like to lose something close. That's what happens when you fuck with Frank Gercio.

Dickhead was taking too long in the shop. Frank was about to go in himself and pop him for being such a slow, fucking idiot. But who would drive? He didn't want to, he'd just wait till they got home.

Then it occurred to him—it was quiet.

The middle of Queens was dead silent. There were no cars, people, or anything. Granted it was 1:00 AM—still, this was fucking Queens!

He heard something faint, a *whoosh*.

Then it was quiet again. Looking out the window of the limo, the tinted glass made it hard to see anything with clarity.

Whoosh.

What the fuck was that?

Whoosh.

This time he heard it even louder.

WHOOSH.

It sounded as if something were right above him.

With a powerful jolt and scream of tearing sheet metal, what appeared to be an enormous horn of a rhino penetrated the roof and tore through the headliner. At first, Frank thought it was going to pierce his head, but it just curled up and clamped on. Two horns burst through the bulletproof windows in a shower of glass. The limo lurched forward, sending Frank sprawling across the carpeted floorboard over the rear facing seat and into the glass divider in the back of the driver's seat, face first. His nose squashed on contact with the glass as he felt the whole car lift off the ground. The rear facing seat and glass divider seemed to be the new bottom of the car as Frank's stomach dropped. He recalled only feeling this way when a plane took off.

Fumbling and struggling, Frank managed to turn his body around. Another horn had appeared in the back window. What lay beyond that was too incredible to believe: a sleek, reptilian tail—*a long-ass fucking tail!* Behind that image was the panoramic skyline of New York getting real small, real fast.

The gun!

Frank kept a .357 Mag in the side door compartment. Unfortunately, the side compartment was now located above his head. The limo was bobbing back and forth like a toy, and all the secret compartments flew open with each jolt. Frank noticed the gun compartment was already open. Putting his hands down, he felt exactly what he wanted to feel: the long cold barrel of his gun.

"Fuck You!" Frank screamed and fired, but quickly remembered why you should never shoot inside a bulletproof car. The bullet ricocheted off the horn, window, side panel, then penetrated the soft tissue of his kneecap.

"Sonofabitch!" he cried.

When he opened his eyes again and saw all the "horns" at once, it suddenly dawned on him: *They're not horns; they're talons.*

Back at the store, Petey came out to an empty parking lot.

•

This was the worst time of the day for Craig, and he wasn't even out of bed yet. Waking up before the alarm went off was, hands down, the most dreaded time imaginable. His body wanted to stay in bed, but at any moment that "click" would go off, followed by awful country music. Craig purposely set the alarm on country because he had to get up to shut it off. Another smart move was placing it on the other side of the room so he physically had to get out of bed to shut it off.

It was still dark out. If God was merciful to him, it was only 2:00 AM. However, since it was the end of August, 2:00 AM and 4:30 AM looked identical outside. For once, his mind was clear. Every once in a while, a good sleep purged all the bad shit out of his head and he could just relax. It was wonderful to feel the softness off the sheets and pillow. At any moment, though, there was going to be a click, then some corncob yodeling. After that came the drive into work on the wonderful Long Island Expressway.

Oh joy of joys, God bless Queens. Maybe it was still 2:00 AM?

Craig had been dreaming, and sometimes when he awoke from a

dream, it seemed like the next day when it was really only two hours later. And it was a wonderful dream—the one where he was flying again. This time it was over the Catskill mountains. Lakes and forested mountainsides passed beneath him as he soared toward the horizon. He was alone. Meredith wasn't with him. Odd. Still the dream was so peaceful it made him feel good and horny as hell. Maybe that's why Meredith wasn't in it.

Ring.

No.

Ring.

No, not the phone! This early, the phone always meant shit had hit the fan. Energy came quickly as wakefulness rushed through Craig's body.

"Hello!" he answered as if he had been up for hours.

"Get that scrawny white butt in here Scalici. Gercio's been hit, I think," Aisha cracked.

"What do you mean 'you think'?" Craig rebuffed.

"I mean get in here now!" Aisha returned.

"Okay, I'm on my way." Craig grunted and pressed the receiver down, then dialed again. It took two rings before Mrs. Snow answered.

"Yes, Craig?" Mrs. Snow answered.

"How did you know it was me?" Craig asked, almost offended.

"Who else would it be? I'll send Jeannine right down," Mrs. Snow responded as she always did.

"I owe you," Craig replied.

"Yeah, the rent. Don't forget," she added and hung up.

Craig lay there for a second, contemplating checking on his daughter before he left. He decided it would be better if he didn't; she might wake up. The radio clicked and Tammy Wynette started to sing.

"Stand by your maaaaan...."

"Ugh," Craig moaned.

•

Aisha Barlow had been Craig's partner for **only** a year and a half. Out of all the detectives they could have placed **her** with, she felt God purposely had a hand in the paring of the two. Nobody made her think like he did. Sometimes she felt like his daughter, sometimes she felt like his wife, but most of the time she felt like his mother. He could handle the shits they went after, and even some of his fellow officers when the need arose. Yet, she still always had the feeling he was like a child lost in the big city. This was her woman's intuition at work; the rest of the men they worked with could not see these qualities in Craig, but she could.

She was worried about him. Gercio was powerful and stupid, a dangerous combination. Craig had the uncanny ability to get under his skin and wrap his nerves in tinfoil. If he wasn't a detective, he would have made a great mob dentist. It also worried her that Craig would push somebody without fear of reprisal. Gercio would push back, and only once. What happened tonight, she felt, was the start of something big. Gercio would not leave this earth without a mechanism in place to get rid off the irritants in his life. Craig was the biggest.

Craig entered the room unshaven with a bad clip-on tie. That was fresh as a daisy in Scalici terms. Aisha sat on her desk enjoying her normal bagel with cream cheese and 7-11 coffee. It could only be 7-11 coffee. The chemical the squad room Mr. Coffee made was toxic, and thus, saved for lawyers. Only two other plain clothes men were in the room. Of course, she had a bagel and coffee for Craig. Lord knows he wouldn't think to get them for himself.

"So what happened? Was Gercio whacked or what?" Craig asked, trying to fix his tie and grabbing the coffee at the same time.

"You're welcome," Aisha said, looking at the coffee.

"Oh, thanks." Craig asked, "Okay, so what happened?"

"Gercio and his limo disappeared from Oscar's Cigar Shop. The driver said he wasn't gone from the car more then two minutes and it disappeared with Gercio in it. According to the driver, Gercio didn't like to drive, and even if he did drive away, it would have taken awhile to maneuver the limo out of the parking lot."

"What about his house, anybody call to see if he was home?" Craig stuffed half the bagel down with one bite.

"Called the house on Staten Island, as well as the girlfriend Tina's apartment. Nothing."

"What about the daughter?" Craig already knew the answer. "Up in Livingston?"

"Once she stopped calling me every racial slur in the book, she said no." Aisha smiled sarcastically.

Craig felt there was something else.

"And why the shit-eating grin?" he asked.

"The driver, Peter Cusamano, he's in the back asking for protection." She smiled wider.

With his mouth half full of bagel and coffee, he let it hang open revealing it for all to see. "He's talking?"

"He wants to talk," she repeated.

Craig looked up and saw the other to men looking on, elated.

"Did you hear that shit?" Craig spoke with food flying out of his mouth. "He's gonna talk!"

The others in the room start to clap.

●

Petey sat in the interrogation room alone. *How could so much go wrong so quickly?* No matter what really happened, Marcella was going to blame him. He was supposed to protect Frank to the death. There was nothing to suggest a hit. There were no cars; they didn't stop at Oscar's on a regular basis. Maybe he wasn't even dead; maybe he just drove off in a rage? But how could he have gotten the limo out of that tight little parking lot so quickly?

Over and over Petey played the evening's events in his mind: He went into the shop. Oscar handed him the Havanas; he didn't have to ask. What else? He remembered thinking he had to get back soon before the boss lost it altogether. The weather was getting bad; he heard the wind picking up. He would have heard the engine start.

I'm being watched, he thought.

Looking at the mirror he could just imagine who was on the other side, gloating. A few hours ago he would have given it the finger; now his life depended on whoever was behind it. A cold draft blew over his hands that sent a chill right up to his jaw, which started to tremble. He felt it wasn't the mirror watching, the whole room was. The door flew open and 250-pound Petey jumped a good foot and a half.

Craig and Aisha walked in. They'd dealt with Petey before he was a major player. Now it was about to pay off. Craig ran right up to him and pinched his checks.

"Petey, if you weren't so butt-ugly I'd kiss ya." Craig laughed.

"You do and I'll belt ya!" Petey shot back.

Craig turned back to Aisha.

"You hear that, Detective Barlow? He threatened me." Craig smiled.

"Heard it loud and clear," Aisha nodded.

Craig turned and put his face right into Petey's, his smile turning into a childlike grin.

"Listen, you fat fuck. The only reason you're here is to save your fat ass from Marcella. When she hears, and she already did, that you let her dad get whacked, your balls are fish food." Craig spoke in his psychopathic child voice, "Now you speak when you're spoken to, or you get no cream puffs after dinner."

Petey just looked at him and nodded.

"Now tell me what happened," Craig said as he backed away.

"Um, I'm want a lawyer here. I'll tell you everything Gercio did, but get me counsel," Petey begged.

Craig stared at him and reality began to raise its head a bit.

Craig's tone became serious. "What scared you, really? Off the record. What makes a big guy like you so nervous? You know we can hide you."

"No you can't. What happened tonight is proof of that," Petey blurted out.

"Explain." Craig sounded almost sympathetic.

"Look at how he fucking disappeared! You fucking noticed?" Petey ranted. "They weren't hit. They just die or disappeared all together."

The detectives gave a quick glance at each other. They knew exactly what he meant. The Gercios never put a contract out on anyone big. Small thugs were taken care of by their soldiers. But bigger fish would unexplainably die or disappear. *The Post* actually started calling him

11

Lucky Gercio.

Aisha asked, "You mean nobody actually killed those people?"

"Not by regular means. But if you ask me, Marcella did it some-how." Petey explained, "If she didn't like you, you were gone. The word was, *she* was the real boss."

"Do you actually think Marcella got rid of Frank?" Craig asked, completely enthralled.

Petey nodded his head.

Aisha noticed how cold it was in the room. She could see breath coming out of the two men's mouths as they spoke. A knock on the door nearly stopped her heart.

"Come in!" she yelled with a heartbeat of at least 120.

One of the officers popped his head in with a bewildered look.

"They found the limo and maybe Gercio," the young officer advised.

"Where?" Craig asked.

"Albany," he answered.

"Albany, New York?" Aisha replied.

"Upstate, New York, Albany," the young cop repeated. "Do you want me to turn the heat up or something? It's freezing in here."

Craig noticed the mirror; it had frost on it.

•

"Wake up, sleepy head," Jeannine's voice called out. "We're going to the beach."

Meredith opened her eyes and saw Jeannine's face, a sight that was more common than her dad's.

"I made some chocolate chip pancakes for ya," Jeannine smiled.

"Did Daddy get called into work early?" the seven year old asked. "I heard the phone ring, then he cursed out the sock draw for not open-ing."

"Yeah, he did, and don't repeat any of those words he used, either. Now get dressed. Once you eat, we can catch the 7:10 bus to the ferry to the beach." Jeannine ruffled Meredith's hair.

Meredith loved it when Jeannine babysat her. She was the coolest, and she was sixteen! She always baked the best cookies, and every time they went out, all the boys came over to talk. Meredith decided that when she got older, she was going to be just like her, and double-date with her. Too bad Daddy wasn't seventeen; they'd be perfect together. Jeannine hopped out of the room in her cool cutoffs with all the fancy embroidery, her braided ponytail bobbing up and down. Meredith couldn't believe that a mean woman like Mrs. Snow could have such a nice daughter. Then again Mrs. Snow's own mom was a nice lady.

Meredith got out of her bed and went to get her favorite bathing suit out of the drawer. Grandma Messinal had given it to her at the beach house. Most of Grandma's gifts were fuddy-duddy, but the bathing suit was just the coolest. None of that Barbie junk was cool; the sunset printed on the suit was *very* cool. She pulled it out, fraying seams and all, leaving the six other suits behind. The smell of the pancakes hit her nose, making her stomach churn in anticipation. The day was going to be just the best.

She soon forgot all about her dream of flying the night before.

•

Craig and Aisha made it to the field in three hours with Craig driving. The trip to Albany usually took four. A dozen state troopers swamped the middle of the field so neither one could see what they were gawking at. Craig didn't bother parking on the side of the road. He drove the car right up to the crowd of troopers, none of whom seemed to care. He got out first and no one approached their car. Craig and Aisha exchanged looks, then he reached in the car and blared the horn. All the troopers jumped and grabbed their guns.

"Yo, by any chance is there someone in charge here?" Craig hollered in his normal sarcastic tone.

The troopers stared at him for a moment then to Aisha. From the cluster, a six-foot-five Lieutenant emerged with a perplexed expression on his face. This was not a man that got frazzled easily; today he was.

"Are you Scally and Barlow?" the lieutenant asked.

"That's Scalici," Craig replied. "Why the huddle?"

The Lieutenant didn't say a word. He just motioned them over. Like the Red Sea, the troopers parted. At first glance the detective thought they were looking at a large tan-gray rock with white spots. Then as they both moved closer, Craig noticed one of the white spots was a cow skull. As he looked closer, he realized the whole mass was nothing but a pile of fur and bones. Like a meteorite, it was imbedded in the ground as if a plane had dropped it.

"Now you tell me detective, have you any clue as to what the hell that thing is?" The lieutenant crossed his arms, thinking: if Kojak here, had the answer, he was hanging up his gun and retiring the next day.

"Beats the shit out of me," Craig answered.

"At least you're honest, Kojak." the lieutenant replied, taking his hat off and scratching his head. "Thirty-three years I've been doing this. I can't begin to explain this."

"Where's the limo?" Aisha asked. "They said you found Frank Gercio's limo."

"Other side ma'am," he said, walking around the twenty-foot lump.

"It looks like a turd," Craig remarked, looking at all the leg bones and skulls. There was even a cowbell in it. He sniffed the air. "It don't smell like shit though."

"Smells like a science room from school," Aisha noted.

The lieutenant stopped dead. "Acid, that's what it is! Acid!" he realized. "*That* would explain it."

"Explain what?" Craig cried in frustration.

The Lieutenant pointed to the lump. Craig and Aisha looked in the mass of fur and saw the back end of the limo. The paint was gone leaving shiny steel reflecting back at them. Surprisingly, the license plate was untouched and read 'Gercio One'.

"Jesus H. Christ!" was the only words to escape Craig's mouth.

He went over to the bumper and grabbed it.

"Don't touch that!" Aisha yelled at him.

"Jesus Christ. It just disappeared last night. When was it found?" Craig asked, in a dream like state.

"Early this morning. Residents say they heard a loud crash around 4:00 AM."

"That's only three hours from the time he disappeared. Anybody check inside?" Craig asked.

"No! If you want to burrow in, Kojak, go right ahead," the lieutenant said, almost laughing. "I'm washing my hands of this. It's all yours."

"That's big of ya, Smokey," Craig shot back.

Something caught Craig's eye. A few feet to the side, there was a little fleck of gold. Something reflected from a cow skull eye socket. Without thinking, Craig walked over and grabbed the skull. His fingers dug deep into the fur around it giving little resistance. To Craig, it felt like a papier-mâché sculpture Meredith made in school. Watching, half the troopers and Aisha winced as Craig stuck his other hand around the skull. He pulled it out sending a cloud of fur in the air. In the open cavity left behind lay the skeletal remains of a human hand, with a gold pinky ring still on it.

"Frank, there you are! Your family's been worried," Craig said in all seriousness.

"Excuse me ma'am," the lieutenant said to Aisha, "but your partner is one strange individual."

"Yes. Yes, he is," she confirmed.

•

By the time Craig and Aisha made it to Albany, Jeannine and Meredith had already been at the beach for several hours. They caught the 7:30 ferry out of Bay Shore across the Great South Bay to Atlantique Beach. Jeannine had taken her there so often; she was even enrolled in the summer camp the town provided.

For Meredith, Jeannine was more then a mother's helper. Since her mother was gone, Jeannine was her replacement mother. She barely remembered what her own mother looked like. Except for the pictures in Grandma and Grandpa's beach house, she only had one memory of her mom. She had been crying because she didn't like her food, so her mommy had slapped her. She did get Christmas and birthday gifts from her, but they were really from Grandma—she could recognize the handwriting. At one o'clock, the camp was going to the Sunken Forest for a nature walk further down the beach. It was right next to Dune's Point where mommy's parents lived, but she knew her dad would get mad if she called them.

"What's on your mind?" Jeannine asked.

Meredith was in her own little world again, eating a big chili dog at the picnic table while Jeannine had gone to get more lemonade. The concession stand guy liked Jeannine and always gave her free food.

"I was wondering if I should call grandma and grandpa." Meredith looked up from her "Lets go Mets" cap.

"You know how your dad feels. He doesn't want them to know that I watch you so often," Jeannine reminded her as she sat on top of the table.

"Do you think my mom is there?" Meredith asked out of the blue.

"Well, since she didn't go there the last time you were over, I doubt it," Jeannine answered, as she chomped down on her own chili dog. Half the content slipped out the other end and landed with a splat on the table.

Immediately both girls started to laugh.

"Eew, that's gross!" Meredith exclaimed.

"Not as gross as this." Jeannine laughed, and poured some of her lemonade on it.

"EEEW!" both of them squealed.

Meredith shivered, which was instantly noticed by Jeannine.

"You okay, squirt?" Jeannine asked

"I'm fine, I just got a chill," Meredith replied, suddenly feeling sick to her stomach.

"You don't look so fine."

"Can I go to the forest now? I don't like it here, somebody's watching me," Meredith said, her voice grave.

"Of course somebody's watching you! Me!" Jeannine replied.

The cold feeling of her being watched vanished and Meredith felt warm and good inside.

"You're the best," Meredith smiled.

"I know." Jeannine smiled back, grabbing Meredith's head and giving her a noogie.

"So let me get this straight," Aisha began with Craig as they crossed over the Tapenzee Bridge. "Gercio was offed by a cattle rancher and dissolved in acid with a herd of cattle."

"No, no, no, it was a symbol of some type. Maybe he had links to the meat packing business that we didn't know about," Craig said, fumbling for an explanation.

"If you believe that, I have some swamp land to sell you," she quipped, rocking her head back and forth.

"You know, I don't care," Craig sang and started to tap his hands on the wheel. "Gercio's gone and Petey is going to put the rest of them in jail."

"You think Petey is going to rat out the whole family?"

"Did you see the look in his eyes? He's terrified. Marcella probably has a contract out on him already."

"You heard what Petey said. They don't put out contracts. Things just happen."

"Things don't 'just happen'," Craig boasted, knowing the answer. "They don't tell people what they're doin'. Then they can't squeal on them."

"What about Marcella?"

"What? I don't care how mean she is. Mob guys will never take orders from a woman. It would be mass castration for them."

"You don't think this whole thing is odd? What the hell was that stuff the limo was in?"

"Some type of fabric or papier-mâché. What? Do you think its some type of voodoo or witchcraft?"

"It's not normal! And before you get your hopes up on Petey, you'd better find out what happened last night."

"So what do you think is more powerful, voodoo or witchcraft?" he asked, pretending to be serious.

God, she hated it when he did that.

"You're gonna have to deal with bitchcraft if you don't watch it," she warned. After a moment she answered, "Voodoo, of course."

"I'd have to disagree," Craig said, edging her on.

"I know you do, even when people are right you do. And I'm going to have to save your ass one of these days because of it."

Craig stayed strangely silent as they approached the tollbooth.

"How did they get him up there?" he asked out loud. "They had to pay tolls?"

"I thought you didn't care?" she said triumphantly.

•

It was a quarter to four by the time they got back the station. If Craig wasn't completely fixated on how Gercio was skeletonized inside of his limo, along with a dozen head of cattle, he would have noticed the lobby and hallway were unusually empty. Aisha thought it odd, especially, to see Devaney by the cooler all by himself.

"Yo, Devaney, where is everyone?" she asked him.

"They're up in Harlem looking to fill our darkey quota," Devaney giggled and sneered.

"Thank the Lord you fill our stupid quota, or your hometown would be milked dry," Aisha dished back. She almost felt bad for Devaney. As her father always said: "You can't have a battle of wits with an unarmed man."

Devaney immediately grabbed his crotch.

"Child, you wish you had them."

She almost felt sorry for him. Devaney was one of the good ol' boys in the precinct. With his crew cut and pressed white shirt, he was the Anti-Craig.

"Did Devaney seem like a bigger prick than normal today?" she asked an oblivious Craig.

"Maybe they used a helicopter?" he thought out loud. "Maybe with a big industrial junkyard magnet mounted on it, they picked it up?"

"Are you in Scalici world again?" she asked rolling her eyes.

"No," he quickly answered. "Devaney's always a big prick!"

Of course Craig made sure he was loud enough to let Devaney hear him. Craig always knew how to get to people with his mouth; rarely did she ever see him use physical force. Yet, unlike others with a quick wit, he was quite capable of backing it up with force. Aisha didn't need Craig to protect her, that's why God invented guns. Devaney though, seemed to be the type to be somewhere else when you needed back up.

The two of them entered the squad room and were immediately surprised. A giant banner reading, "CONGRATULATIONS," was sprawled across the back wall. The room was filled with all of the other officers of the precinct, and cases of beer stacked on the desk. All at once they began to applaud.

"What the fuck is this?" Craig blurted, never being one for couth.

"Just shut your trap and appreciate it!" yelled Chip.

Chip O'Hanlen was Craig's best friend from the academy; before Craig's daughter Meredith was born, they were inseparable. To Craig, that was a lifetime ago. For Chip, it seemed like last month. With the exception of Aisha, Chip was the person closest to Craig, and stood up for him many times. Even though they were all in the same brotherhood, Chip found it harder and harder to get his cohorts to remember Craig the way he was. It almost came to blows with Devaney trying to get the party off the ground.

"I don't know about my sidekick here, but I want some cake!" Aisha said as she moved past Craig.

"Baby, we got devil's food cake just for you," Chip said, lifting a devil's food cake off one of the desks.

"Chip, if I weren't married with three kids, I'd make you my wife," Aisha joked. Chip was one of the few in the precinct she actually felt comfortable with.

"I'm all yours baby." Chip joked back.

Chapter 2

THE LADY WAITS

The ferry ride home seemed to take forever. What took only twenty minutes in the morning always felt like an hour and a half in the late afternoon. Meredith clenched her final science project for camp. She had to make her very first oral report on her results. Visions of Earth-shattering discoveries ran through her head as she envisioned herself in another ten years or so. Thus, many secrets that only her superior scientific mind could sort out, were placed in her Barbie bag. Jeannine was beside the bench talking to two of the lifeguards who had been at the beach. Even Meredith could tell what flirting was; nevertheless, Jeannine would always give her a quick wink to let her know she was keeping an eye on her.

The rattle of the old Fire Island Queen vibrated harder and harder as it trudged across the bay. Meredith didn't like having her teeth shaking in her head like that, especially after a hard day at the beach and camp.

20

As the ferry made its last turn into Bayshore, the sun shone directly on her face. A summer's worth of tanning had made her impervious to pain so all she felt was warmth. She sat and watched all the high school kids making out and rolling their own shiny cigarettes. They were all just the coolest.

Bitch!

A voice spoke in her head. Meredith looked around as the weird feeling from before came back to her. An icy ribbon of cold ran up her back, as if an ice cold thread was being placed there, wrapping itself around her neck.

That's weird, she thought.

It tightened around her like a noose.

All at once, Meredith couldn't breath. Dropping her bag, she immediately put her hands around her throat. Under her fingers she could actually feel an icy ring around her neck.

Relax, she told herself, *it's all in your head.*

The grip grew tighter.

She tried to yell for help, but no words came out. Her head grew fuzzy and she felt as if it were going to explode.

"Meredith?" Jeannine's voice came to her through the haze. "Are you okay?"

Immediately the cold ribbon disappeared and the sun's warmth bathed her again. She looked up to see her babysitter standing over her with the lifeguards looking on. Meredith took a deep gasp and began to cough.

"I was just holding my breath, just like Shirley Babasoff did in the Olympics," Meredith lied.

"She was swimming at the time, and she didn't hold her breath!" Jeannine scolded.

"I'm sorry."

"You're tired! And your dad's gonna have my head if he finds out you're depriving yourself of oxygen!"

"I won't do it again," she said, knowing it was the voice that tried to choke her.

"What do ya mean, you're splitting?" Chip asked, more annoyed than questioning.

"I got to get home! Plain and simple!" Craig repeated.

"Buddy, the whole world knows what a good father you are. But this is ridiculous. You don't know the time I had getting this party off the ground," Chip emphasized.

"And I appreciate it. But I have to get home, you know how she is," Craig explained, putting on his jacket.

"I have an idea. I'm her godfather. Can't you take some time for yourself?" Chip began to scold, "Like it or not, you have a family here, too. And they don't like getting the cold shoulder. You can take the time to celebrate at least once with them, show them you're one of them."

"Neither one of us are in our twenties anymore. They can go beering it up tonight with my blessing. Hell, send me the tab, but my daughter comes first."

"My kids come first too, always will. But listen to me buddy; hang out for just an hour more. You and Aisha did a phenomenal job, let them show some respect."

"Why don't you take Aisha out? She did half the work," Craig suggested in an obvious set up.

Without saying a word, Chip grimaced. "But she's not one of the guys. It would be like guzzling with your mother."

"Well, at least you're not raciest, just a sexist," Craig sneered.

"And you're ungrateful. We're your friends, too, remember?" Chip shot back.

"Not all of you," Craig pointed out. "Please, go out, and the first two rounds are on me."

"Don't do this, buddy."

Craig started for the door, looking at his watch. Most of the heads in the room turned and saw him leave, including Aisha. The volume immediately began to wane as if a knob had lowered their voices. Aisha acted quickly to minimize the frost.

"Chip, did you make a pass at him again?" Aisha cracked.

"No way, hon. I'm saving it all for you," he bantered back.

The quick distraction helped alleviate the already tense situation. The group did manage to go ahead and go out on the town without the man of honor. Unfortunately the man of honor had given them cold shoulder one too many times.

•

At 5:30 Craig was still stuck on the Long Island Expressway, not an uncommon event. He waited and looked around at the other cars surrounding him. All the people looked so oblivious to all the crud around them. None of them knew what an evil world was out there. Like many of his fellow officers, Craig was going to raise his family as far away from the NYC shit pile as he could.

Glancing out the car's window, he saw the body of a dead cat on the side of the road. Half its guts were hanging out of its mouth. Flies were feasting on the remains. Up to now there were only two thoughts in his head: getting home to Meredith, and how did they get that limo upstate? For the life of him he couldn't fathom why he didn't think of it before when he found it. Was he so obsessed with nailing Gercio that he didn't care how he was taken care of? He had seen some sick shit over the years; body parts sent UPS, bodies nailed to front doors. There was even the head of Juan Salicear found in a sealed bag of manure. Gangsters went to great lengths not to merely kill a man, but prove a point in how it was done. To think that someone would go through such great lengths meant that a very big point was being made.

But to whom?

Gercio was the top man. All the others fell in line behind him. As a matter of fact, he kept such a tight hold that *no one* dared challenge him.

Marcella.

Gercio's only child was his daughter Marcella Zimmer. The gist of most insiders was that she was an insane daddy's girl. She always got what she wanted from him. Every jaw dropped in the precinct when they found out she married a Jew. Never in a million years did anyone think the goddaughter would be permitted to marry a non-Catholic, much less a nice Jewish boy. Wills must have clashed with her dad, and she had won. Now that Daddy was dead, maybe she might actually take his place.

Never.

No, women didn't belong to the mob, let alone run it. Only someone insane, soulless, and ruthless could ascend. Then it dawn on him, Marcella fit all of the above.

The traffic started to move again. From the corner of his eye, Craig saw movement. Just as he let the car begin to roll forward, he looked back at the dead cat. A large seagull had it in its grasp and was trying to fly off with it.

God, get me to retirement.

•

At 6:15 Craig pulled into the driveway of the house they called home, a three-story gray Victorian, with a wrap-around porch. He rented the entire bottom floor from the ever-smoking Julie Snow. If he could retire at the young age of forty-one, Mrs. Snow said she would consider selling him the whole house. Already he and Meredith had free reign of the tremendous yard, and Mrs. Snow and her mother were like a built in Aunt and Grandmother for Meredith. The daughter, Jennine, helping out was just icing on the cake. No matter how bad things got at work, Craig was truly happy with his home life. Unlike everyone else he knew, Craig also had the ability to leave his work back in the City at the end of the day. Only in the wee hours of the morning did it begin to seep back into his brain. Nothing, but nothing, was going to violate his perfect home life.

The sun's rays felt warm and soft as they caressed Craig's bare face as he exited the car. He had been teleported safely back to wonderland. Meredith sat cross-legged on the back patio picnic table, busy taking something apart. Up on the porch, eighty-something year-old Mrs. McIlvain, sat rocking in her chair reading the *National Inquirer*. Her Inquiring mind wanted to know things. Like always, a can of Tab sat next to her with a half-full glass. "You should never drink from a can," was her sentiment. "It's not proper."

"Evening, Mom," Craig called to her while taking off his jacket.

"Evening Detective," she smiled back. "Solve any mysteries today?"

To this day, Craig still loved being called Detective. It gave him a hard-on, even from his adopted grandmother, yet he'd never admit it.

"As a matter of fact, I did. Any more alien sightings?" he inquired, pointing to the paper.

"Just up in the Catskills again. They've been getting a lot of them lately," she replied matter-of-factly, peering over the paper.

"Hum, have they abducted any mobsters?"

"No, no monsters."

Craig laughed and went to Meredith sitting on the table.

"No 'hello' young lady? Been waiting that long?" he asked, releasing the tie from his neck.

She looked up with a smile. All memories of the ferry ride were put aside in her child's mind for another time.

"Hi, Daddy. I'm working on my science project for camp."

On the table, in front of her knees, were two gray furry pellets. In her hands were the remains of a third.

"You'd rather destroy lint balls than kiss me?" he asked, bending down to her face.

Meredith stopped and gave her dad a peck on the cheek.

"They're not lint balls, silly. They're owl pellets," she corrected him. In her hands she showed him not only a mound of fur, but also a half dozen tiny bones. A tiny skull looked back at him from her tiny palm.

"You see, owls eat the mice whole, but they can't digest the fur and bones. So they puke it up in one big pellet."

Before his eyes, Craig saw an exact miniature of what he'd seen upstate. He took one of the remaining pellets and sniffed it. No odor at all.

"We're out of glue. I need to stick the bones back together on paper tonight. Can you get some?"

The request fell on deaf ears. Unable to control his thoughts, Craig felt in his gut that somehow Gercio had met the same fate as the mice. But that was impossible. No way could anyone mimic something like this—not on this scale—especially the dumb shits in the families. There had to be a meaning. Yeah, as ridiculous as it was to try and fathom, Gercio and his limo were eaten and then puked up in the world's largest owl pellet.

"No way!" he told himself out loud.

"But, Daddy?" Meredith cried, " I *need* glue, tape won't work!"

Craig's thoughts instantly went back to his child.

"Oh, not that, darling. I'll get some glue when I go get the pizza."

"Great! But don't get that crappy stuff Mrs. Snow gets."

"Meredith Ann!"

"Well she always lends me the cheap glue, and it's not the same!"

"That's not what I mean!"

"Oh, 'crappy' is a bad word?"

"Yes. Where did you hear it?"

"The beach, Uncle Chip's, Aunt Aisha's, but mostly Mrs. Snow."

Craig shook his head. Sometimes he thought he was the last adult on the planet that didn't curse in front of children.

"Well, it's a bad word, and I don't want to hear it. Now if you go inside and order the pizza, we could eat in half an hour."

"Okay, but don't forget, you promised to play monopoly with me."

"Of course. But after you're done with the remains, um, pellets."

"Okay, José."

Craig started to help his daughter off the table, only to have her hop off and dash toward the door. On the porch, Mrs. McIlvain was gone, along with her paper. A warm summer breeze was the only thing keeping Craig company. The rustle of the leaves in the trees above had a soothing affect on his body. He wanted to just lie in the soft grass on the lawn and stare at the clouds. In the wind, he could hear a high pitch sound, a very familiar sound, of the engine of Mrs. Snow's '62 Chevy. It wasn't a piercing sound, just one so familiar that he could always tune into it. In the back of his head he always wondered how far away she could be and still pick up the sound of that one rocker arm off kilter. Timing it perfectly, he turned around to see the immense battle green car pull into the driveway beside his. It was the same familiar sight: a cigarette perched in her upper lip as her hands grabbed over each other, turning the hula hoop-sized steering wheel.

She must have the arms of a truck driver to steer that thing. Lord knows she had the mouth.

Julie Snow was from the old country, Brooklyn. For as sweet as her mother was, Mrs. Snow took no crap from anybody. If it ever came to blows, even Aisha would be no match. But like Aisha, she'd make sure you were fed before she'd crack your head.

"Well look at what the tide washed in," Mrs. Snow muttered while lugging out two full bags of groceries.

"Good evening, madam. How was charm school today?"

"Watch it, bub."

"Can I give you a hand?"

"Nah, I got it." The cigarette bobbed up and down in her lip. "Heard about your friend Gercio on the news. I'm not gonna have any mob guy shooting the place up am I?"

Click, Craig's mind began to turn.

"What did you hear?" he asked once again letting the realities of his job seep in.

"That he disappeared last night and his skeleton was found up near Buffalo this morning." Mrs. Snow said, walking up to the door. "Sounds like you have some leaks in your department."

Craig felt the anxiety swell in his gut. This was going to get worse. Whoever took out Gercio made more of a mess then already existed. It was well known that he had it in for Craig, and the good people of the news ate it up. Nobody from the TV or the mob ever came by the house, but there might now be a *big* spotlight on him personally. Maybe he could get in a few hours of quality time with Meredith, but he knew the phone would be ringing soon.

It was who was on the other end that was the big surprise.

•

"Fucking Asshole! Fucking Asshole!" Marcella repeated over and over almost in a chant as she paced back and forth in her living room, each thud from her 250 pound body rocking the house to its foundation.

27

The place was swarming with her men—her father's men the day before. The other bosses had been calling her all day to offer their condolences, and to assure her that they had nothing to do with whacking her dad. This fact she already knew. She was waiting to get Petey in her grasp and find out exactly what he saw. Things had gone completely crazy and she did not have the control she'd like. *Fucking Asshole* was involved somehow, she knew it and felt it. The entire day she tried to piece together the cluster fuck the night before. Even when she tried to take someone out that afternoon, it fucked up. Fucking Asshole fucked that up too! She heard a car pulling up the driveway. If they didn't have Petey with them, she was going to fry all of their asses.

A loud rap came from the door. Since she threw everyone outside, she was even more pissed having to answer the door by herself. Swinging it open, Benny stood there alone as the others cringed. Fear shown in all their faces, something she always liked to see.

"Where is he?" she demanded.

"We can't get to him. They keep moving him."

Marcella spun on her heel and thundered back into her living room. Benny knew this meant to follow. Half the men gave the sign of the cross as he entered her lair.

"I want a meeting with Dad's council!" she commanded in her tremendous pink silk robe.

"Mrs. Z., with all due respect, they'd never give you an audience," Benny reminded her.

"They will after I find Petey," she said coldly. "As long as I can find him alone!"

"Scalici and Barlow gave strict orders and..."

Benny did a no-no—mentioning their names in her house. There weren't too many guys who could intimidate Benny, but this hulking monster in pink sent a chill straight down his spine, right out his asshole.

"All I need is to find out where he is," she said calmly. "Just tell me where he is. Unless *you* can tell me what happened to my father?"

"I have to tell ya, Marcella," he confessed, "this is the weirdest fucking thing I ever saw."

Marcella went right up to his face. "You haven't seen nuttin' yet."

"Mommy!" Georgy's voice called from upstairs, turning Marcella's demeanor to something almost soft.

"In a minute dear, mommy's busy." She turned to Benny, "Find Petey, or I'll cut your balls off."

"Yes Mrs. Z."

"And keep an eye on my husband. Whoever did this may try to do the same to him," she added as she marched to the stairs. "Mommy's coming sweetie."

•

By 8:30, Craig and Meredith had reduced their pizza to a few remnants of crust. As Meredith finished gluing her archeological finds to powder blue construction paper, Craig checked in with the precinct. He'd left specific orders on how to keep Petey out of view of his cohorts. The officer on the phone busted his chops about not going out with the rest of the boys; Craig quickly lectured him about parental responsibilities. It seemed Petey was terrified and actually wanted to be flown out of the country. Craig didn't feel sorry for Petey; anyone who willingly led a life where you kill innocent people deserved to be terrified. Still, Petey could give them all the information they needed to bust up all of the Gercio family and others.

Craig hung up the phone and wondered how long it was going to be before someone would call. If there was anything to do with the Gercios, a news reporter would eventually get to him. Never at home though.

"Meredith, why don't you get the Monopoly board?" he asked her.

"Sure thing!" She jumped up and ran to her room.

Curiously, Craig walked over to her project. Three tiny mouse skeletons were glued to the paper with surgical precision.

She's going to be an Orthopedist.

Laughing out loud, the thought that a giant owl ate Gercio and his limo was hilarious. There must have been something in his past and going on in the mob to have them do this. The style of his death meant something to someone.

I hope.

The phone rang and almost caused his heart to explode.

They've found me.

Craig answered, hoping it would be Aisha or Chip. "Hello."

"Craig?" a woman's voice asked.

Craig's racing heart stopped dead.

"Trisha?" he asked, knowing who it was.

"How's Meredith?"

"Um, fine. You missed her birthday."

"I know. I was in China believe it or not. I forgot."

"Your mother sent her a gift, again. But I think Meredith's getting wise to it," he said with the hair rising up on the back of his neck. "Why are you calling?"

"I wanted to talk to you, actually."

For a moment, Craig felt bad. He figured she must have seen some news reports and pieced things together.

"I'm sorry, thanks for calling," he apologized.

"I saw the news up in Hartford and came down immediately."

"Thank you. I wish it was under other circumstances."

"Oh the circumstances are perfect, I'm suing you for custody."

•

Tanya and Jerry rode the special patrol that night. Fresh out of the uniform and in plain clothes OCCB (organized crime control bureau), Tanya was all of 105 pounds. Jerry, on the other hand, was a seasoned veteran at the ripe old age of thirty-four. He was pissed when he learned he was getting a female rookie. He wanted a photocopy of himself, or of his retired partner, Henry. Instead, he got one of the city's attempts to make all things happy and politically correct. No scoping out babes with this one in the car. No bar hopping and tailgate parties with her! Oh no, he had to be the sucker "Poster Partner."

Both Craig and Aisha asked them for this special favor. The way the department worked, they could get away with it. In the back seat, wearing a fake black Afro wig, sat Petey, as the OCCB officers took him on an all-expense paid tour of Manhattan. It was Aisha's idea for the wig. Their orders were to drive around the entire shift, then meet up with Chip in Jamaica. Since Jerry was the senior officer, rock music was to be blasted until midnight. After that Tanya would get to blast disco until dawn. Their mission was not just to protect Petey, but to make him as miserable as possible.

"Would you two little shits turn that crap down!" Petey protested from the back seat.

"Why, this is Led Zeppelin my good man. You have to hear it as if you're in the Garden to fully appreciate it!" Jerry explained turning it up even louder.

"You're all a bunch of freaks. Especially that Scalici ass-wipe!"

"And gunning people down in bagel shops is normal?" Tanya threw back, endearing herself to Jerry already.

"Look at you. At least cops used to be men! Fucking fags! Listening to that shit! Letting niggers and cunts on the force."

With that, Jerry slammed on the brakes, stopping the car immediately. The momentum catapulted both Tanya and Petey forward. Without the benefit of a seat belt, Tanya slammed into the dash. If she hadn't brought her arm up, she would have cracked a rib for sure. On the other hand, Petey's face hit the screen partition at 30 mph. The Afro would have worked as a cushion if they were only going 10. His nose was pulverized as Jerry immediately sped down an ally, Led Zeppelin still blasting.

"What are you doing?" Tanya yelled, as Jerry flew out the door and pulled Petey out of the car.

"What the fuck did you say?" Jerry yelled, throwing Petey down and making a fist.

"Jerry no!" Tanya screamed, running to stop him.

"What the fuck did you say?" Jerry repeated, his eyes bulging with rage.

"You and your cum hole are a bunch of fags and lesbos!" Petey snapped, in hopes Jerry would take the bait. He didn't mind getting hit, as long as he could get in one good shot of his own.

Tanya immediately got between them, spoiling Petey's plan.

"Stop it! We can already get in deep shit as it is. Don't make it worse." Tanya begged him. "He can't testify with a broken jaw."

"Oh, I don't have to break his jaw!" Jerry responded surging forward again.

Tanya shoved back and grabbed his jaw.

"Go get a coffee for us! Take a walk around the corner and cool down!"

"I'm not leaving you alone with him!"

"What's he gonna do? He can't go anywhere! He's stuck with us," she reminded him.

Jerry retreated back to the street.

"Fuck you, you faggot pig!" Petey yelled, taunting.

Jerry stopped. Tanya didn't know if she could stop him from attacking the star witness a second time. He looked down, shook his head in dismay and walked out to the street. Tanya turned around and kicked Petey hard in the gut.

"That's for the 'C' word!" she yelled and kicked him again. "That's for the 'N' word."

"You bitch!" he sneered back.

Tanya turned off the music and the sound of the police radio took over.

"Now get back in the car and put your seat belt on."

Petey looked at the blood on his hands from his nose and climbed back inside the car as Tanya slammed the door behind him. Suddenly she noticed how cold it was; they had apparently found a cold spot in an otherwise warm summer night.

Petey watched Tanya go to the street looking for Jerry. That was good. That crap they were listing to was now off, and he actually preferred the sound of the police radio. The same monotone woman's voice would come on with a click, then a series of codes. Then it went silent.

Halla-fucking-luia!

It clicked on and the same woman's voice came out over the radio again.

"There you are Petey!" it spoke.

Immediately he thought it was Lick-Me and Dick-Me playing with the radio. But he could see her and she wasn't using her radio. Dick-Me's voice was too deep to sound like that.

"Did you honestly think you'd gotten away from me?"

"H...h...who are you?" Petey asked, looking around for someone nearby with a walkie-talkie.

"Don't bother looking around. I'm in the radio," the voice responded.

Petey reached for a door handle, but there was none.

"You can't get out. You're in the back of a police car," the voice said. The little green light on the radio stayed on as if to watch him.

"Get back here!" he yelled in Tanya's direction.

The radio laughed at him, a high pitched woman's laugh.

"You know, I don't like the "C" word either."

Petey couldn't talk as fear gripped his chest.

When Tanya returned to the unusually quiet car, she felt proud of herself for preventing Jerry from killing Petey. "You're lucky Petey, you ought to thank me—" She stopped cold.

Something white.

Through the darkness of the windshield, Tanya noticed something white in the back seat.

What the fuck?

She stepped closer and saw Petey arched in the back seat, unmoving. Not knowing what to make of it, she walked up to the window for a closer look. In the back seat, Petey was frozen with his back arched and one hand clutching his throat. His other hand was hooked onto the mesh partition, actually bending it. Every hair visible on his body was pure white. From the thick crop on his head, to the five o'clock shadow, it was a brilliant white. She looked at his eyes, open wide and still. The pupils opened almost as much the irises. His face looked as it was made of wax and pulled back like a cartoon character screaming.

She stood there a good five minutes before Jerry returned with coffee for all three of them.

Chapter 3

THE BITCH IS BACK

In all the years Craig lived below her, Julie Snow never once heard a peep out of him. Craig's voice was now vibrating Hummels off her mantelpiece. After a good forty minutes, she went down to the apartment below. Knowing it was none of her business, she also knew that Craig would never survive without her support. She hesitated before knocking; the vulgarities out of Craig's mouth didn't waver a bit.

"Who the hell do you think you are anyway? No court in the world would give custody to an abandoning slut like you!" Craig's voice resonated, then paused for the response.

The door opened slowly and Meredith stood there with tears in her eyes. Julie Snow knew what was going on. Hell, the whole neighborhood knew at this point, but she asked the child anyway. "Honey, what's going on?"

"Mommy called. I think she wants custard." Meredith sniffed.

"Custard?" Julie scowled, knowing Meredith knew better.

"I think she wants me back."

"Listen, why don't you go upstairs and watch TV. Mom's in bed, and Jeannine is at a party."

"Okay. Can I watch HBO?" she asked, since her dad didn't believe in cable TV.

"Sure thing, just don't put on anything bad," she promptly instructed, knowing *The Way We Were* was the only thing on for the eightieth time.

Meredith went up the steps and Julie marched in. Craig was still yelling at the phone. Julie immediately got his attention and gave the sign to cut it out. Craig glared at her then muzzled the phone.

"What do you want?" Craig snapped.

"Shut your goddamn mouth! Your daughter's upstairs crying. If you haven't noticed, she gone!" Julie threw right back at him.

Craig quickly looked around, and then went back to the phone.

"I don't care who your father hired, you're not getting her!" He seethed in a more controlled voice. Again he looked around for Meredith. Julie pointed upstairs.

"I don't have time to—" Craig stopped and winced. "Operator, I already have an important call... Yes, yes put her through... Aisha this is not... Oh shit!... What *happened*? ...Where are they now? ...Has anybody talked to them? ...I'll be right in. Trish, you still there? ...As you can hear...what do you mean you heard enough?" Craig said without breathing once.

A loud click was heard and the room went silent. Julie could not believe everything she just witnessed.

"Don't worry about Meredith. I'm sorry for butting in..." Julie began.

"God no, um, thanks," Craig answered, dazed. "I don't know what I'd do if it weren't for you?"

"Go clean up the shit that obviously hit the fan. Meredith will be fine." Then her curiosity grew. "If you don't mind me asking, what's going on?"

"Well, filthy rich ex-wife has decided to remarry and become a full time mother, and two rookie cops apparently scared my star witness to death," Craig blurted out with a neurotic smile.

"I'd say you're going to be putting in some overtime."

Craig pulled out his keys and unlocked the drawer under the phone.

"Do me a favor, if any lawyers or reporters come by the house, don't talk to them. Matter of fact, don't talk to anyone." He took his revolver out.

"Don't worry. Besides being gorgeous, I have brains too," she quipped as Craig rushed out.

"You're the best!" he yelled back.

•

When Craig and Meredith first began eating their pizza, Aisha got the first call. She never did get to leave the precinct that night. Hubby was home with the kids, and the boys in blue actually wanted to give her her due. She was not one for beer, yet anything with vodka was okay with her. One by one, many of her cohorts came up to her at Flannery's and paid their respects. All of the ones who did so were the ones that did not care that she was black or a woman, the latter being the more threatening. She could pretty much tell who was racist and who wasn't. Unfortunately, the good people didn't want to rock the boat when a-holes like Devaney acted up.

Two months ago, even her "friends" would not have taken her out. Then again, anyone who expected almost 400 years of ignorance to evaporate in just a decade needed a good jolt of reality. It felt nice that these men were here to celebrate with her. She even felt comfortable in their presence. Chip was always a little cold, jealous that Craig was getting a new best friend. But even he started to lighten up a bit, which was good, because Craig was beginning to isolate himself from his co-workers. Unlike the movies, being the lone wolf in this job was not smart. You needed to run with the pack whether you liked it or not. Craig was beginning to run away. She knew she needed to have a talk with him.

The bar itself was comfortable now. When they first got there, Chip felt a definite chill in the air. Blaming it on the air conditioner at first, he later passed it off as psychological tension from Craig not being there. He and Craig had closed the place down many a time, and still showed up for work the next day. They made a lot of friends back then, thank God. He found those bonds that Craig forged was the only thing helping him now. Most people didn't realize that Craig was just being overprotective of his kid and not looking down on them.

Behind the bar, Decklin, who'd been bartending for cops since the 1940's, was holding up the phone scanning the crowd.

"Who they lookin' for Deck?" Chip called out, expecting a wife looking for a husband that promised to be home hours ago.

"Aye, who's Detective Barlow?" Decklin asked in his thick brogue.

"Oh, I think it's the black chick," Aisha called out, sending a roar of laughter from the boys.

Decklin frowned at first, then realized, and handed the phone over.

"Barlow here," Aisha answered.

From across the room, Chip saw her face lose all color.

"Where are they?" she asked.

With no one else noticing, Chip made his way over.

"I'll be right there," she said, tossing the phone back to Decklin.

"What is it?" Chip asked, grabbing her shoulder.

"Just come with me. I don't know what to expect."

Perplexed, the two gave no goodbyes and ran out, with Devaney watching from across the street.

•

Craig reached the alleyway at 9:54 PM. By the grace of God there were no news reporters there. There were certain codes to be used on the radio so the press wouldn't pick it up on their scanners. On the other hand, there were more police cars on the scene than at the St. Patrick's parade, plus two EMS ambulances. The secret wouldn't be kept for long. Every single head turned and looked at him as he ran out of the car. A hundred sets of eyes glared down to his soul, and he felt every one of them.

"Any of our guys down?" rushed out of his mouth before he came to a full stop.

"Just the oil spot," someone called out, referring to Petey.

As Craig approached the patrol car, the paramedics were wheeling the gurney to the street. The large mound underneath the blanket was unmistakable. Petey.

"Aisha!" Craig called out.

"Back here," her voice answered away from the street.

"What the hell happened here?"

"Christ, I don't know! He got scared to death?"

"Heart attack?"

As the medics were passing, Aisha stopped them. "Pard' me guys." She grabbed the blanket and pulled it back. Petey's snow white face stared back at her. All the officers standing around gossiping stopped as dead as Petey's lifeless body. It was the expression on his face that chilled everyone, including Craig.

"Holy Shit!" was the only thing Craig could say. "Are you sure it's him?"

"Right down to the white pubic hair," Aisha replied, pulling the blanket back farther.

"Holy Shit!"

"Is that all you are going to say?"

"Did someone try to whack him?"

"Nope. Apparently he got under Jerry's skin. Tanya made him take a walk and was left alone with him," Aisha explained as they wheeled Petey away.

"*Tanya* did this?" Craig asked in disbelief.

"Well, she left him in the car only two or three minutes. When she came back, he was whiter than Barry Manilow."

"What's the coroner saying? Why aren't they here?" Craig asked, looking around at the mayhem.

"They were here. They said heart attack. I think his face tells us how it happened."

"Where's Jerry and Tanya now? They okay?" This was the more important answer to Craig.

"Jerry's a little rattled, but Tanya's a little bit in shock. She's in the rig with some O-2. I put Jerry in the diner across the street."

"Anyone talk to them?" he asked.

"Just me and Chip."

Over her shoulder he could see Tanya sitting in the back of the ambulance, wrapped in a blanket.

"Do me a favor, run blocker for me out here. I smell news turkeys on the way."

"Better them than internal."

Craig looked at the visual barbs being slung at him. Even the medics were giving him the evil eye.

"I don't know, I just don't have the feeling I'll have the backing I should," he said, taking note of the glares of his fellow officers.

"It's about time you caught on."

"They're this pissed because I wouldn't go out drinking with them?" He approached the ambulance.

"It's more than that."

"Great! They're worse than Trish!"

Aisha stopped dead her tracts. He had spoken the forbidden name.

"Hold on there, partner. What…"

"Yup, she was the one on the phone when you called. Excuse me if I start flipping out and shooting people."

Craig sped ahead leaving Aisha with one thought: *Holy Shit!*

•

Despite the warm summer temperature, Tanya was shivering in the back of the ambulance. Sitting on the bench, all she wanted was a hot cup of chicken noodle soup. The medics tried to get her to lie down. To her that would have been too much of a final insult. She knew she wasn't going into shock, she was just cold, and summarily told them to leave her alone. She was grateful they listened and didn't try to pick her up.

"Hey tenderfoot, hear ya used too much bleach on Petey back there," Craig greeted her with a smile.

Tanya only knew Craig a short time, but already knew he had a gift to calm things. Shaking, she looked at his warm eyes looking back at her. Immediately the chill began to slip away.

"D-d-detective. I think I m-m-messed up," she stuttered, still feeling some of the cold.

"What'd ya do, show him a picture of Devaney in a thong?" he asked with a straight face.

Her muddled head was not capable of a snappy come back at that moment, so she gave him a smile. Climbing in the ambulance, Craig bumped his head on the padded door frame.

"Damn it! Fucking Oompa-Loompas built this."

He seated himself next to her and asked her to repeat everything that happened.

"And there was nothing else?" he asked.

"Nothin'," she said, looking at him with confusion in her eyes, then adding, "Well, one thing."

"What? Tell me everything."

"Do you think he could have frozen to death?" she blurted out. "I know what it looks like, but he looked so cold. I got a chill too. Like I walked into an ice box."

"Froze to death? You don't even have air conditioning in those patrol cars."

All the chill was now gone from her body and she found herself able to chuckle.

"I'm sure they'll find out what happened after the autopsy," he reassured her. Then, looking around first, he leaned closer to her. She could feel the warmth of his body on her cheeks. The smell of pizza was still on his breath as he whispered. "If anybody asks, this was all my idea. I intimidated you into doing this."

Before she could even gasp and protest, he glared at her with those eyes of his. She knew he was right. He was much better adapted to fend off and attacks than she was.

"Yes sir," she agreed. "I never should have left him alone. If I hadn't your star witness would still be alive."

"Or whatever scared him to death could have scared you too."

Tanya shook her head. "How's Jerry?"

"He's fine, I'm going to check on him now."

•

Chip and Jerry sat alone in the diner. Even the counter boy knew not to stay in the room and went in the back, not eager to hear what was going on. All he knew was that they had fucked up big time, and he didn't want to be called as a witness.

Craig walked in the propped-open door and saw the opposite of Tanya. Jerry was sweating profusely. His short-sleeved, pale blue shirt was now dark navy and dripping. He held a bag of ice cubes, now almost water, on his head as he sat in the first booth. Chip stood over him like a doting mother fearing the worst. His jacket was off, also showing huge sweat marks. The two men looked to Craig as if they were holding their breath for his arrival.

"Jesus, what did you do? Fly here?" Chip asked.

"Kirk gave me a lift. Tell me what happened? Any brass show yet?" Craig asked, already knowing the story, but more concerned how he was going to explain it all.

Chip replied, "No one big has wind of it yet. I was waiting for you to show before we cleaned house."

Craig sat down in the booth across from Jerry, resting his arm in some dried sticky leftover on the tabletop.

Fucking great. It just keeps getting better and better.

Jerry let out a breath and told his version of the events. Just as Craig feared, no new light was shed on anything.

"I'm telling you, if I had played it cool with that grease ball, none of this would have happened," Jerry growled, then slammed the booth with his hand.

"So you got a temper! We all do! You think you could have prevented this?"

"Damn straight!"

"You were going to stop a heart attack?" Craig threw out with just the right amount of sarcasm to let Jerry know that this was going to be the official version of events, and to let him know there was nothing that could have been done. Once again, Craig managed to calm the storm brewing in someone's head.

Jerry's anger immediately began to lessen. "But what the fuck scared him?"

Craig looked to Chip in a desperate attempt for an answer. Chip responded with an "I don't know" shrug.

"Maybe he thought of Marcella naked," Chip suggested. "Hell, I'd be shocked white from that."

Jerry smiled, noticing the gleam in Craig's eye.

"What is it, sir?" Jerry asked.

"Chip is right. You know how scared Petey was of Marcella. You know how he refused to stay in one place for more then twenty minutes. The way he insisted on being driven around all night with that wig on."

"I ditched the wig, sir," Jerry noted.

"Good! Anyway, you know how I told you to do this, even though it was against policy," Craig continued to coach.

"But the overtime was needed for your rent," Chip added with the same gleam.

Jerry picked up on everything.

"With that fat bitch after me, I could be scared to death, too," Jerry said, nodding.

"So would I," Chip agreed.

"And don't forget, I told you to do this," Craig said in conclusion.

"Actually, I'm the one that relayed..."

"No! I, and I alone, gave you the order to do this. Not Aisha, not Chip, it was me."

"But sir, I—"

"No buts! This is *my* wonderful mess," Craig insisted.

Jerry and Chip gave each other a glance and knew almost telepathically that this was how it was going to be. On top of everything else, they also knew Craig always got his way. They were both very happy he was their friend.

Craig pointed toward the ambulance outside. "Now go check on your partner."

Things seemed to be somewhat under control. It was then that Craig noticed Jerry's tattoo. Half the men in the precinct had them, but it was the eyes staring back at him that called his attention. On Jerry's ample bicep was a dragon. Its red eyes stared out from a long green body. Its long tail wrapped around his arm in a circle. In its jaws, being devoured, lay a smaller dragon's limp body, its eyes shut as blood dripped from his wounds.

"Nice tattoo, Jerry. A bit gruesome, don't ya think?" Craig commented, completely enamored by it.

"It's from when I was in the Army," Jerry explained. "My whole company got them. I think it intimidates the perps more."

"It intimidates me." Craig shook his head in awe, then turned his attention back on Jerry's face. "Look, if the news comes calling, wear long sleeves. Understand?"

"Sure thing, but I thought nothing intimated you," Jerry replied, already self-consciously covering his tattoo with his hand.

"Wait 'til you meet my ex. Actually, maybe she was the one who scared Petey to death."

All three laughed as Jerry got up and walked out to the ambulance. Putting his hat back on with confidence, all his self-doubt seemed to be gone.

"Man, you're a work of art, friend." Chip smiled. "You definitely have the golden tongue."

"I'm going to need it, too. Besides this shit, she called me tonight." Craig said all in one breath.

"No fucking way…" Chip knew who "she" was immediately.

"Yes, way. And on top of that, we never got a statement from Petey. Come on, let's help Aisha clean up." Craig laughed, grinning a toothy smile. "Maybe we can get it all done before Dr. Bellows and Mrs. Brady get here."

•

Most of the cops were gone when the first news crew showed up. Their enormous van with its satellite dish always reminded Craig of a bad science-fiction prop, ready to shoot a death beam at network competition. The tow truck was pulling Jerry and Tanya's patrol car away as the space van from channel hell parked in front of the diner. Petey's body was already gone.

Thank God.

Trent Gold, field reporter, was out of the passenger's seat before the driver could even put the van in park. Aisha was the first one who caught his eye. As the star-roving reporter, he had already learned to always head for the female officer. They couldn't resist him. He had also learned to stay away from Craig, who had slipped over to the ambulance where Jerry and Tanya were.

"Excuse me, detective. Trent Gold, Live Action News. We understand there's been a break in the Gercio case." Trent thrust a mike in Aisha's face.

Aisha barely had time to inhale before she was dowsed in bright light and a camera lens.

"Um, no comment. Please refer all questions to DCPI," she instructed, tempted to go for her revolver instead.

Trent Gold Live Action News flung the mike back to his mouth. "Is it true that Peter Cusamano, a-k-a Big Petey, was going to testify against the Gercio crime family? And did he not suffer a fatal heart attack moments ago?"

"Again, please refer all questions to the Department Commission for Public Information," Aisha repeated, trying to look as professional as possible.

"Could he have been poisoned to silence his testimony?" Trent threw back, along with his mike.

"Again, Mr. Gold, no comments at this time."

By that time Craig had convinced the ambulance to pull away without its lights and sirens on.

"Detective, it's been this reporter's experience that 'no comment' is another way of stating 'cover-up.'"

"Again, please..." she spoke with the voice of exhaustion.

"Trent!" Craig's voice interrupted. "How are ya? Did you forget I'm the only one with DCPI clearance to talk about Gercio?"

Craig had doubled around the back of the Live Action News squad.

God Craig! Don't weird out on TV! Aisha was worried.

"Detective Scalici. Can you tell us what has taken place here?" Trent inquired twirling around to Craig.

"Rather than tell you, why don't we have a look? It's worth a thousand words. Right?" Craig asked with a straight face. Aisha could always recognize when Craig was keeping a straight face.

"Why yes, Detective, it certainly is," Trent replied.

From in the diner, Chip also saw the disaster in the making. It was like watching a car sliding on the ice. You could see the wreckage beforehand, but weren't able to do a damn thing about it. Craig was herding them over to the alley.

"Detective, how did you feel last week when Gercio openly threatened you?" Trent snuck in, as they were led to the alley.

"Now, now, he didn't openly threaten me personally. He said, 'That wonder bread wop was going to get it.' If he had specifically named me, I could have arrested him," he pointed out in his fake lawyer voice. "Now don't go putting words in his mouth. It's all right to glamorize him, but don't lie."

They reached the alley where the cameraman illuminated the dark corridor, revealing the trash and filth in the shadows.

"And what are we supposed to see, Detective?" Trent asked, beginning to realize he was playing into Craig's hands and knowing he had to see it through without looking like a complete ass. If he had to, he'd have to embarrass the psychopath on film. Nobody would get away with mocking him on his own news show. He knew he shouldn't have gone live. But Channel Seven would be here in five minutes.

"Well it's not down there, Trent. Look up at the roof," Craig announced in his official police voice.

Before Trent could signal the cameraman not to go for it, he flung the light up to the top of the buildings.

"And what are we supposed to see? A diversion from the truth?" Trent tried to recover.

"No, a blimp. A big magical blimp with little monkey pilots." Again in all seriousness.

"What happened here detective?" Trent yelled while positioning his face for the camera.

Craig put his arm around Trent.

"I'm just joshing ya, Trent," Craig answered, then looked right into the lens. "We're old buddies, really."

Aisha just stood there. The near twenty-four hours that she had been up was now culminating to this. The odd thing was, Craig once again seemed to be getting control of the situation. She just hoped he wasn't having a nervous breakdown in the process.

Chip also had similar concerns, but saw an opportunity to get Craig away from them. He approached them. He did not want to be put on camera, but who knew what would come out of his mouth?

"Are you hiding the fact that your star witness was scared to death? That his hair was shocked white?" Trent boiled.

"Scared white? You see folks, he such a card," Craig taunted sarcastically. "He's great. I think the national news should get him. Make sure you call and tell them to get Trent."

Trent realized his situation, but desperately didn't want to let it show that he was losing control. If he pressed the man any further, he could make matters worse.

"In all seriousness Trent, we cannot discuss things at this time. We will contact you and Live Action News as soon as possible."

"Detective!" Chip called out. "You're needed on the phone."

The camera turned, shining directly at Chip.

"Why thank you, Detective," Craig answered, then turned back to Trent. "I have to run. Duty calls."

Immediately Trent Gold turned his face to the camera and began to cover. "As you see folks, something as taken place here, and we will keep you informed as developments unfold. Now, back to Ned in the newsroom. Ned."

The Camera light turned off at the same time Trent's face knotted into a snarl. Looking up to the street, he saw all the police cars pulling away. Each one had an arm out, giving him the finger. He wanted to get that jerk so bad. By the diner, he saw the other two detectives climbing into a sedan. Standing beside it, he saw Scalici staring back at him. His eyes almost seemed to be glowing. He could see every detail of the irises as if he were standing face to face with him.

The world went silent in Trent's head. *He'd kill me if he could get away with it.*

"Would you get in the car?" the woman detective scolded Scalici. Unflinching Craig continued to stare at Trent, then silently got in the car.

At first, the thought of revenge was ridiculous. But as the detectives' car drove away, so did Trent's fear of Scalici.

Time to dig, asshole.

•

To Craig's amazement, sleep came easily. With everything running through his mind, he thought he'd be wired for a week and a half. Foremost in his mind was whether or not to call home. It made more sense to stay at Chip's house in Brooklyn than drive back to Islip. He wanted desperately to call Mrs. Snow, but he figured there really was no need. He told Aisha to go home and not to come in until noon. Lord knows, she'd been up longer than he had.

It had been quite a while since he'd been to Chip's house. The last time was a christening, and he had forgotten which kid it was for. Something else to lament over. Chip put him up in the guest room and went off to bed himself. Craig hoped he got the chance to see Barbara in the morning. God, he almost forgot what she looked liked.

With all the thoughts mish-mashing in his brain, Craig no sooner shut his eyes than he went right to sleep. It was a very sound sleep.

Then he began to fly.

He was first over Brooklyn, then headed north across the sound. Little by little the buildings below began to give way to trees. The air flowing around him was warm, like bathwater that was just right. Looking down, the trees below slowly went from leafy hardwoods to tall pine trees. He began to climb higher in the sky. Facing the moon, he looked at his hands and arms in the light. To him his skin still looked as if it was that of a child. Pale and white, he could see all his birthmarks that he had growing up, the unique little blemishes that stayed with him like long lost brothers and sisters.

He thought about Jerry's tattoo, the dragon. He remembered its shape and the smaller dragon being devoured. The larger dragon's claws were gnarled and twisted and ready to shred its prey. Craig looked down at his own body. Without being startled or phased in the least, he saw that he himself was in the grasp of a giant claw. Completely unaware of it until that moment, it felt more like being held by a blankets.

Of course, it's a dream.

On either side of him he could see the massive leathern wings gracefully drift down then up like they were floating in water. He couldn't see its head, or turn to see the back. But he knew what would be there, a huge head and long tail, just like on the tattoo.

Yet different.

This was a female—a female dragon flying with him, carrying him high into the sky. Passing clouds, he felt a soft arousal in his gut, something he never felt for Trish. The claw around him suddenly tightened as if she didn't even want him to think of Trish. He did anyway. He thought about how he had never loved her, and how they only married because she got pregnant.

The grip loosened a bit.

Can you read my mind? He asked with his thoughts.

No. She answered back gently with hers.

Chapter 4

POST MORTEM

Craig woke up at six o'clock sharp, invigorated. By 6:10 he was showered and dressed in one of Chip's suits. In the kitchen, Barbara was cooking up breakfast wrapped in a worn terry cloth robe older than all her kids. The room itself was a tribute to the color avocado green. All the appliances were green, along with the tablecloth and curtains. Yellow flowered magnets were stuck to the refrigerator door with a marker board missing its magic marker. The string just dangled there with its empty loop waiting for the pen's return. Above the sink was her plaque that proudly announced, "Barbara's Kitchen." At the table, Chip sat with a cigarette in one hand and a mug of coffee in the other. Neither eye was open; his clothes seemed to have been flung on. Unlike Craig, Chip was still in dreamland.

"Morning, Barb, how'd sleeping ugly make out last night?" Craig asked giving her a peck on the cheek.

Barb gave him a once-over. "Excuse me, but do I know you?"

"I'm sorry, Trent Gold, dead action news. I'm reporting on your husband's alertness." He came back cocking his brow with a dead on impersonation.

"He didn't sleep well, tossed all night. Is he on the case with you?" she asked, getting back to making pancakes.

"No, he decided to help Aisha out 'til I got there."

"Well tell him to stop, he has his *own* case load."

Craig immediately got the hint. "Can I borrow the phone?"

"She's fine, Craig. I called your landlord two minutes ago. I didn't think you'd be up this early. And look at you, all bright-eyed and bushy-tailed."

"I'm always bright and bushy. Can I call anyway?" he asked again.

"You don't have to ask, go ahead. Even though you haven't been here since Sammy's christening you're still welcome," she reminded him in a frosted way.

Sammy, that's it!

"It's manners, you should always ask," he replied, picking up the avocado phone.

"So's calling once in awhile. Then again, I don't see the lump over there that often either."

"I plan it that way," Chip croaked.

Upstairs Craig could hear the rumblings of the O'Hanlen horde. Again he couldn't remember the kids' names. It had been way too long. Meredith would enjoy playing with her near cousins. That's if the bitch didn't steal her. The phone rang once and Meredith's voice answered the phone.

"Daddy!" her voice rang out.

"Morning, darling? How was your night?"

"Great, Jeannine slept over. She's taking me to the beach in a bit."

"What a surprise. Now I wanted to talk to you. Remember what I said about strangers?"

"Mrs. Snow already reminded me. Don't talk to strangers."

"Very good."

"Even if they have a lost puppy," she added

"Right."

"Even the rat bastards from the news."

"Ah yes, but don't call them that."

"Love you, Daddy."

"Love you too, dear. Bye, bye, and don't give Jeannine any trouble. See you tonight. I owe you a monopoly game," he tried to squeeze in before he heard her hang up.

"Who would have thought that you'd turn out to be a mush-dad?" Barbara joked as she slipped the pancakes into their plates.

"I would have," he replied, seating himself in front of the grub. "Wake up buddy, you have bad guys to catch."

"Fuck 'em, I feel like crap."

•

"You know, you start school next week," Jeannine said to Meredith while they waited for the ferry.

By itself, that wouldn't have put Meredith in a bad mood, but there was the memory of the boat ride home the day before. She didn't tell her dad, he seemed to be busy with mom and work. The opening that she had entered so many times before seemed to be swallowing people one by one as they willingly entered. The Fire Island Queen was really a big monster eating people and spitting out their bones like the owl pellets.

"Meredith, what's wrong?" Jeannine asked. She always said Meredith, instead of kid, when she was serious.

"I don't want to get on the boat," she said very softly so as not to tell the ferry.

"Does this have anything to do with what happened yesterday?"

Meredith looked at the science project in her hand and nodded.

"You told me you were holding your breath. Was that the truth?"

"No, I think someone was choking me. Someone with very cold hands."

"Choking you? I was watching you the whole time. No one was choking you," Jeannine said crossly. "Were you eating ice cream?"

"Yes."

51

Jeannine crouched down to her eye level.

"Well, when you eat ice cream too quick on a hot day, sometimes your body cramps up, like in the water," Jeannine explained without seeing any calming of her fear. "Look, I'm right here. If anyone touches you, they'll have to come through me. I'm a fourth degree black belt, ya know."

"Are not!" Meredith perked up.

"Am too!" Jeannine insisted, putting her hands up like a karate commercial.

"Can we sit up on top then? I don't want to be inside her."

"Sure, kid."

With that, Jeannine took the girl's hand and marched her on to the old Queen.

•

"I'm interested in the post mortem," Craig said to Chip on the way to work. "I want to see how they dissolved his flesh off."

"Jesus, Craig, the brass is going to roast you after that stunt last night."

"I thought I handled it rather well," Craig said, drinking his coffee and driving.

"You insulted a reporter on live TV. You don't think that's going to piss people off?"

"It's the delivery, old pal. If you're likeable and fun, people go along with it. This morning, if they're talking about last night, they'll concentrate on me and not on Petey."

"That's another thing. So what do you think scared him?" Chip asked with his most cognitive thought of the morning.

"I don't know? Fear of repercussion? I just wish I'd got him to tell us more."

"And what about Trish?"

"Damn that bitch!" Craig thundered. "You had to bring that up! I was feeling good for some bizarre reason, and you had to fuck it up!"

"Sorry. It was just weird that you looked and felt so good."

"Well, fuck you, too!"

"I saw that look you gave Trent Gold, and it scared me," Chip reminded him, now regretting the can of worms he'd opened.

"That ass announced to the world that Gercio was out to get me! Who knows what type of crap that can lead to? And he keeps conveniently popping up right whenever shit happens. So you know it has to be Devaney!"

"He wouldn't dare!" Chip shot back. "He might be a dick, but he'd never—"

"Never what? I swear, I think he'd kill Aisha if he thought he could get away with it," he grunted.

"Listen, Craig, that mindset you had two minutes ago, go back to it," Chip pleaded, rubbing his temples.

Surprising even to himself, Craig remembered the warm flowing flight from the night before—that weird dream he couldn't quite bring into focus. His ability to put things in an orderly perspective began to trickle back. Although, he wondered how quick it would be to fly back home.

•

Chip was not the only one who didn't sleep well. Trent Gold did not sleep at all. At first he was out for blood. When he was in college as Trenton Goldberg, nobody took him seriously. Maybe that's what drove him to adopt the character he had now. No matter what he had to endure, going back to reunions as top dog was worth it. It wasn't cool in his high school and college days to be a geek. When he did start showing signs of succeeding, he was 6'2" and 150 pounds. It was then that he discovered others did not like the token nerd surpassing them.

At first, he couldn't believe that his "friends" would actually do anything to purposely undermine him. That was before he found the demo tape. For some reason he decided to view it one last time before he mailed it in to the network that was interested. He knew every second of it. The way he looked with his contacts in, and a little muscle he had built up made him feel, well, sexy. Being well-spoken and intelligent made it all the better. He remembered wrapping the old style mag tape in the video machine (years before VCRs and DVD players) and sat back to see his accomplishment one last time before he sent it to Buffalo's P.M. Magazine.

What flickered on the screen was a test video he'd done his freshmen year. With his thick glasses and pizza face he looked like the poster boy for adolescence. However, it was the stammer in his voice that was the worst. The voice of being unsure and scared. It was no surprise to him that he wasn't the most popular, but to be hated so for just doing better then the rest of them was heartbreaking. Luckily, he had a spare copy of the tape on file—the same file they must have snagged the freshmen film from. Sure enough, when he went to get the copy, he saw they had taken that first year horror show of his. He was half expecting the good tape to be gone, too. Long story short, he got the job. It wasn't long after that he landed the Live Action News position, and had been enjoying the limelight ever since. He had built a reputation for helping other news people get started, a reputation that helped him get every one of his friends blackballed from the profession.

Trent did not appreciate Scalici taunting him on camera like that. It brought back too many bad memories. He wouldn't even have been there if this Devaney jerk hadn't insisted that it was going to blow the lid off the Gercio case. Devaney was always right in the past when it came to Gercio and Scalici. But there was something more there than just a cop cracking the mob. Somehow Scalici was able to ferret out every move Gercio made. He was either the luckiest man on the force, or he had an ace up his sleeve.

Often, Trent actually found Scalici a better story than Gercio. But he kept his distance from him. He knew he was a live wire. One did not make it to the ranks that he had without knowing how to deal with people who get in your way. So Trent did his best to stay out of Craig's fire. If he wasn't such a good story, he would have gladly left him alone all together. He could have made the black woman a star in the media's eye. Yet there was something about Gercio and Scalici that made them so compelling. Now Gercio was gone, and Scalici, who he personally admired, was now on the list with his former "friends." To make matters worse, or better, depending on how one looked at it, the ratings for that night were horrible. Almost every TV in New York was tuned to the Mets-Yankee game.

So if nobody saw it, why am I so pissed off?

It was the embarrassment, he realized. He had been in control, and he didn't like being reminded of the time when he wasn't. Maybe the man had a point. Putting his name on the news like that was not a good idea. But most people loved it.

Still, he poured over the old videos on the Gercio case. All night long he wanted to find something to give the evening news to run. They had no interest in his fuck up. Just as he was about to put the whole episode behind him, he took one last look at the alley film from the night before.

"A blimp, a big magical blimp with monkey pilots," Craig's voice returned again.

Hatred for that wacko filled Trent's insides again. That sarcastic tone in Craig's voice still managed to eat his nerves raw. Looking at the video, he witnessed the cameraman's screw up all over again. He should have known not to listen to him. There it was in all its glory, a brick wall. How much airtime has ever been wasted on a bare brick wall? He wondered if there was anything here to salvage.

That's when he saw it.

An eye. Right above the roof was an image of an eye. Immediately, he reversed the film. It disappeared, then reappeared when he forwarded it again. At first he thought it might have been a reflection of his own on the glass, but it froze when he stopped the tape. It almost looked like an x-ray of an eyeball. The pupil was white with a dark thick rim around it. The white of the eyeball was a dark shade of gray. He had an eerie feeling while looking at the white veins crisscrossing it like a road map on the gray field.

And it didn't just disappear. It closed. It blinked into thin air. Back and forth he played it, again and again it opened and closed before his own eyes.

•

"Do you think they had to piece the skeleton back together?" Meredith asked Jeannine.

Mortified, she looked down at the young girl staring up at her. The air was just a little bit cooler that morning as they rode on the upper deck of the ferry; it matched the tone that seemed to have been set. Jeannine wanted to go back to the lower deck, but knew Meredith would protest.

"It's a bit chilly up here. Sure you don't want to go back downstairs?"

"No! Do you think the doctors are gluing that Boss Gercio guy back together? You know, that guy that threatened my dad?" Meredith persisted.

"I don't know. Now how did you know about that?" Jeannine asked, thinking they did a good job keeping her oblivious.

"I think they had to. Like what I did to the mouse bones," Meredith answered matter-of-factly.

"Meredith, how did you know about that man and what he said?"

"I saw him on the news at your place. Besides, the kids at camp tell me everything. What type of glue do you think they'd use?"

Jeannine was at a loss. She thought they had shielded her well. Apparently not. She felt like she was caught in a lie in a big way. Although she hadn't lied, she had deceived the child. That's one thing she herself hated, being deceived. So many people deceive for someone else's "own good." And there were so many deceptions that children had to find out on their own. People always wondered why younger people distrust older people. This was one reason why, for we all deceive our children in one form or another.

"I don't know, maybe Elmer's?" Jeannine answered honestly.

"What about this other guy, Petey? I don't think Aunt Aisha scared him to death, do you?"

"Who knows? Maybe he just died?"

"Get real, Jeannine!"

"Well! Maybe it was your mother?" Jeannine blurted out. That woman had been on her mind more than anyone or anything else. Now it slipped out.

"Maybe. She scares Daddy."

"Nothing scares your dad."

"Mom does, she always has."

•

"What?" Craig asked again.

"Ah, all the soft tissue has been removed," Dr. Albequrk repeated. "Even the brain within the cranial cavity."

Craig stood there in the morgue with the Turkish pathologist, the best the M.E. had. "How could this have been done?"

"Ah, either the body was devoured by beetles or it was placed in acid."

The answer was not what concerned Craig. It was the fact that he had all ready thought of it. Everyone at one time comes up with a weird explanation for unusual things. When you find out though, that your own strange thoughts are right, it's time to worry.

"Ah, it also looks as if it was placed in a tank with cattle and other livestock. There are traces of animal hair throughout the remains. I have not had a chance to study the animal remains as of yet," the doctor added, looking down at the complete skeleton on the stainless steel slab. Every single bone that had once been Frank Gercio just over a day before was spread out like a puzzle.

Craig had dealt with Dr. Albequrk many times before. The lime green tiled room had become as common as his own kitchen, including the box of doughnuts and coffee pot on the counter. With any of the other pathologists, he would have held back from asking weird questions. If they started spreading bad gossip about you, it could destroy a reputation.

"Doctor, could he have been digested? I know that sounds crazy."

"Ah, actually that's *exactly* what happened to him. You're not going to see it on my report though."

"Why not? That is your finding, isn't it?"

Albequrk grinned and pulled off his gloves. "Ah, and what will happen to *my* reputation if I said something like that? I'll state what is before us, but I'm not going to speculate. Let someone else say it, then maybe I'll back them up."

"This is a nightmare. Could it have been made to look like he was digested?"

"Ah, anything could be made to look like anything. But how did they compress all the remains into one big mass?" the doctor asked, hunting for his favorite type of doughnut, Boston cream.

"I don't know, what type of animal could digest fucking limousines and fucking cows and horses?"

"Well, my grandmother always told me stories about dragons eating people."

The surrealism was now taken to an even higher level. Once again dragons came up in his life. Albequrk found his pastry and devoured in almost one bite.

"Wait a minute! You're telling me a dragon ate him and puked him out?"

"No! I never said that!" the doctor quickly corrected, with a clear voice and looking at him eye to eye. "Now have a doughnut and pour a cup of coffee and listen to me."

Somewhat surprised, Craig shut his mouth, a rarity in itself. He poured a cup from the pot, grabbed a chocolate glazed doughnut. The doctor shoved a stool over, then offered him a quart of creamer. He started realizing images of fatherly talks that he never received as a child.

"Ah, first let me give you some fatherly advice. When something like this occurs in your life, walk away." The elder doctor spoke pouring his own cream into his mug.

"Walk away?"

"Yes. Ah, what you have here is one of those things that are better left alone. Throughout your life, you will come across things such as this. Naturally, your mind wants to solve this mystery. In the end though, it destroys you."

"Doc, we have to find out what did this."

"Why? Ah, what's the point? A scumbag is gone. I know our faiths tell us to hold all life sacred. Then you look at that man over there.

58

Something decided that we are better off without him. We did not kill him, we did not wish him dead, but now he is. Concentrate on problems that are still problems. Let it rest."

This was unheard of to Craig. "I can't do that, Doc. Now what did your grandmother say about dragons?"

Albequrk answered more like a grandfather. "Fairy tales, dear fellow, only fairy tales. What ate people in fairy tales? Dragons and wolves."

Craig was disappointed. For a slight moment he thought he was going to get some incredible secret revealed to him. Instead, he was being told to look the other way.

Albequrk must have read this in Craig's face and slipped back to being the seasoned pathologist close to retirement again. "Cause of death is homicide of an undetermined nature. The body was then disposed of in acid. Positive ID was from dental records. No attempt was made to alter any of the dental work."

"So they, or it, wanted us to find him?" Craig asked, sensing he got all he could from the doctor.

"Or just didn't care."

"What about the body last night, Cusamano?"

"Ah, I wouldn't know. The body was released to the family this morning."

"What? Please tell me you're joking?"

"Ah, no."

"Doc! How could you just let it go?"

"It wasn't me. He was gone by the time I got here. Wouldn't be the first screw up around here." Dr. Albequrk took off his apron. He almost looked like a morbid deli counter man getting off for lunch.

"Didn't you see him?"

"Ah, if he was gone, ahhh no."

"All his hair was white. I mean *all* his hair. And his face had this twisted..." Craig twisted his own face in an impression "...expression of horror."

"Ah, I've heard of it, but never saw it myself."

"What could cause a terror like that?"

Albequrk looked over to Gercio's remains, then back to Craig.

59

•

Aisha first woke up at 5:30 AM, her normal time. It was a full five seconds before she realized that she didn't have to go in until later. Like most of the people involved with Gercio, she too, did not sleep well. Normally, she would have stayed up and gone into work anyway, but she was *soooo* tired. Germaine had already been up and out. He had a cushy Suffolk county highway patrol job that was twice her pay and half the hassle. She'd always been the early bird, and he the night owl. How they got three kids still boggled her mind once in awhile. Normally, she would have been up and out the door. The kids could always fend for themselves; it instilled independence and got her off the hook. Normally she was a ball of energy and neat as a catholic schoolmarm. But this was not a normal day.

All night her mind raced with repeating flashes of Gercio's skeleton and Petey's scared face. All of her thoughts would merge at once, then take a personal twist. Images of the skeleton lying next to her instead of Germaine, of her bed being in the alleyway where Petey died. By 5:30 she was more exhausted than when she first went to bed. Without a second thought she closed her eyes again. Before she knew it, her eyes flung open to see it was now one in the afternoon. She grabbed the phone and called in.

No answer.

"Damn it!" she yelled and made a dash to the shower.

Who cares if I'm late, I have a perfect attendance, she told herself. *If they don't like it, fuck 'em!*

But it *did* bother her. She always thought of herself as the consummate professional. You show up no matter what. You only use sick days if you can't drag yourself out of bed. Sick time was not free time.

After the last of the suds were washed off, she was out of the shower and back to the bedroom. Thank God for their own bathroom.

"Mom!" Little Ellery called up—Little Ellery who was now six-foot-four. "Mom, where's the syrup?"

"In the fridge, sweetie," she yelled back while trying to get her pantyhose on.

"I don't see it, mom," he yelled back.

"Then try looking!" she answered, continuing the mad dash to get her clothes on.

"It's not there!"

She knew that was coming. "I don't have time to look sweetie, use powdered sugar!" she called out, throwing on the last part of her brown pantsuit.

"I don't want sugar!" she heard him say, coming up the stairs.

Now that she had enough clothes on, she escaped from her room. She didn't have enough time to show her darling middle son where he could put his syrup.

"Mom?" he called from the hall as she grabbed the doorknob.

"What is your problem?" she yelled as she opened the door to see Gercio's skeleton standing there. It stared at her with it open bony sockets, their openings for the optic nerve clearly seen on the backside. With his pinky ring still on, it threw up its skeletal hands and wrapped them around her neck.

Aisha's eyes flew open again, this time the clock read 8:45 AM, just the time she had wanted to get up. Still exhausted, she decided it was better to get up and relax with a cup of tea, rather than attempt sleep again.

•

Provenzono's was the last limo to pull up to Marcella's mansion. She watched it pull up alongside all of the others from her perch in the attic window. She wanted them gathered sooner, but the damn M.E.'s office wouldn't release Poppa's body. It would have been much better to have them over for a funeral, rather than a memorial service. It was taking too long. Her window of opportunity would close soon; otherwise she'd have to start over from scratch. She did not want to flex muscle; it was bad for business.

From his car, old man Provenzono, "Juno" as Poppa would call him, stared up at the house Marcella called home. She could tell by the look in his eyes that he was impressed, very impressed. Things were already working the way she wanted.

She had sent Gregory off to the zoo with his father, something else she would have to contend with soon. Tim was not around as much as he should be. He hadn't made love to her in over a month and a half. Most of all, he did not have the same look about him. Fucking around on her was absurd—he wouldn't dare! No, something else was up with her dear husband. Something she needed to look into. There was a knock on the attic door.

"Mrs. Z," Benny's voice called from behind the door, "everyone is here."

"Perfect," she said to herself.

•

All of the Chiefs were in the dining room. Moviegoers and wanna-be's called them Dons or Bosses, but Poppa always called them Chiefs. All of their soldiers stayed in the living room and patrolled the grounds. Of course there was no need for this at Marcella's. Her place was well protected. They came expecting to give condolences, and maybe find out who was responsible for offing Gercio. They would want to give their condolences, and then keep their distance. They were all interested on how it was done. At that point, everybody in the room knew as much about the skeleton and Petey as Aisha and Chip. Each man had seen a lot in his reign, never something like this.

The wooden doors slid open and Marcella walked in with Benny behind. Dressed in black silk, she appeared radiant. All the men in the room stopped talking at once as the large woman glided in like a cat.

"Gentlemen, so good of you to come on such short notice," she said softly.

"Anything for Francis' little girl," Provenzono answered showing all his respect.

"Thank you, Juno," she responded, knowing only her dad could call him like that.

The room remained silent with what would have been taken as a blatant sign of disrespect. If it had been a son instead of a daughter, it would have been a sign of aggression. Then again the men from the old school could see she was a distraught woman, in deep mourning. She was obviously reaching out to a father figure. If any of the younger soldiers were in the room, they would have gotten antsy, for they all knew, Marcella was more dangerous than any of her male counter parts.

"I wish we could be here to put Poppa to rest, but the bastards still won't release him. They're holding him prisoner in that awful place," she sobbed.

Benny didn't dare roll his eyes.

"I'll call in some favors," old man Terrell assured her. "They owe me big time."

"Oh thank you, Lou. Poppa would appreciate it." She smiled. "Now I have something very important to talk about."

She took Juno's hands and looked to everyone in the room.

"Someone here is responsible for the death of my father. Once I find out who it is, I will kill him myself and all of his family."

The room remained silent.

"As for poppa's business, I am taking full control," she said coolly. "And I expect full compliance with all deals and past practices."

"Marcella, you must be in shock." Juno offered a comforting smile. "Why don't you rest a day or so? We'll talk, you and I, when you're in more control."

Marcella fixed her black eyes square on the old man's face, and then began to squeeze. The frail bones in her grasp were no match for her. Juno Provenzono, eighty-nine years on the earth, fell to his knees.

"Let go! You're breaking my hands!" he cried.

The other Chiefs started for them and Benny pulled his gun and pointed it at the lot of them.

"Get in here! It's a hit!" Terrell screamed.

"The walls are soundproof." Marcella informed them. "No one will hear you. And if they did, I have three times the manpower in the woods and throughout the house. I can kill you all right now, and this far away from any town; nobody of importance will hear the gunshots."

"You always were a bitch!" a sniveling Juno snapped.

"Damn straight! And if any of you doubt what I say, ask your own men. The ones that aren't scared of me, have agreed to work for me." Marcella released the old man from her clutches.

On his knees, Juno looked at his crushed, deformed hands. "Look what you did!"

"That's nothing compared to what's going to happen to my father's killer! Whoever helps me find those responsible, will benefit immensely."

"What about that cop?" Palumbo spoke up. "You stand here and blame us, your family, but what about Scalici?"

Marcella remained still as her father's biggest competitor caught all their attention.

"My sources tell me he's a real stoon-gots. When your dad talked about him on TV, he went ape shit. And I'm told he's not one to back down from a threat."

"I know that fucking asshole. He's the one responsible for Petey!"

By now Benny had already replaced his gun, very happy he was not Craig Scalici.

Chapter 5

THE COMPLETE BOOK OF DRAGONS

After spending the morning with Dr. Albequrk, Craig met up with a not-so-rested Aisha. The entire squad room was under the weather. The party atmosphere was as dead as Petey.

"Has the almighty Barlow succumbed to old age?" Craig asked, handing her the lunch salad he picked up for her.

"Do you want a bullet hole in the head?" She grabbed the bag from his hand and gave him the finger. "This better be diet dressing!"

"Would I poison you with something that tastes good?" he asked melodramatically, chomping on his chili-cheese dog.

"In a heartbeat!" she replied, watching him stuff his face. "Don't you ever gain weight?"

"Nah, not since college."

Aisha looked down at her salad and could have sworn that it looked back at her. "Where'd you get this? A compost pile?"

"I got it fresh from the deli."

She pulled out the bag and showed him a brown withered heap.

"Honestly, it was green ten minutes ago."

She dropped it in the pail as Craig reached into his own bag.

"Don't offer me one of those fat bean tubes you suck down. That could clog up a rhino's plumbing."

"Okay, more for me."

"Heard from Trish?" she asked, putting lightheartedness aside.

"Not yet, but I talked to some of the D.A. guys."

"And?"

"She doesn't have a prayer. She abandoned Meredith and me, has a drug history, and hasn't made contact in over five years."

"She also has money! Lot's o' money! And she *is* the mother," she pointed out, hating every moment of it.

Craig just sat there and stared at his dog.

"Craig, I'm getting worried about you."

There, she'd said it. She had been meaning to for a while, and now was the perfect time to bring things up. "I think you're withdrawing too much into your own world. I don't think you understand what is going on around you," she added, gearing up for more.

"Oh! Do tell me Obi-wan."

"Do you realize most of the precinct hates you?"

"What? Just because I don't go guzzling with them, fuck them!"

Aisha looked around the room. She saw no one watching, but felt everyone listing. That last part didn't help matters much.

"No, it's not just that. People feel you're looking down on them. You used to be one of the pack."

"I'm still part of the *pack*. I'm also a single father!"

"Congrats, I'll give you your sainthood crown! The rest of us unworthies will bow in your aura."

The whole room went silent. Unknowingly, she endeared herself to many of her comrades. But Aisha could not believe what she had just said to her partner, to her best friend. She waited for what felt like an hour, but was in reality only tense prolonged moments, before he reacted.

Eventually, he did, in that cold way about him that could put a chill in anyone. "Thank you, Detective. I always appreciate honesty in moments such as this."

"Craig, listen to me. There is a very good chance that Trish could get custody. You have to realize that. With everything that's going on here now, it'll put you in a bad position in the eyes of a family judge. I think you should take yourself off the case."

No response.

"I know it means a lot to you, but this has the potential of exploding in your face. You may not be able to charm yourself out of the next Gercio, or the next Petey. If Trisha gets a big time lawyer, he'll make you look like a stressed out cop that's losing it."

Again she waited.

"I look around here, and I'm the only one who's not stressed out," he said nicely.

"You *should* be, that would be normal." *Oops!* She didn't mean to say it like that.

"I see," is all he said, and then left, leaving his food behind.

Aisha felt she had just ripped out her own heart. There was nothing like popping the bubble of a loved one.

•

Am I going nuts? Maybe I am? Craig thought, as he walked down the sidewalk.

At that point maybe he was in one big state of denial. Hell, if everybody around you is telling you you're arrogant and crazy, you must be. What he thought was one of his good qualities now turns out to be bad. Was he spending too much time with Meredith? She didn't seem too heartbroken on the phone. He thought everyone respected him. Were they all just being polite? Was he losing his marbles? Damn, and hour ago he was actually asking an M.E. if Gercio was digested by a dragon.

I must be nuts!

Craig stopped and looked at his reflection in a store window. Behind him he could see all the sane normal people walking and shopping. It was another beautiful day in the blue sky behind him. Meredith must be out at camp by now and tanning with Jeannine, he immediately thought. He looked close at his reflection. Not bad for an old geezer. Wouldn't put him a day over twenty-eight. The lines had started around the eyes, the gray in the temples.

This is what's nuts! Listen to yourself pal; thinking like this will make you crazy.

That's when his eyes adjusted to the darker window in front of him. Before him were two red eyes where his had been, around them were green scales with blue tips. It was a dragon staring back at him.

Jesus!

He found himself in front of a bookstore. The book staring at him had a large dragon on it with beautiful calligraphy, curving and winding. It took a minute before he could read it.

The Complete Book of Dragons by Christina Lee.

Captivated, he studied the drawing. Its eyes seemed so real, familiar even. Then, with all the self-doubt crap out of his head, he entered the store.

•

It was a perfect day for it. The sky was clear and the wind was low. The pilot was ready to go at any moment. She could not believe she was going through with it. Growing up, she always said she would never willingly jump from an airplane. Now Gordon actually got her to try it. Skydiving was the thing to do in the Hamptons that summer, and who was she to argue.

What fun it would be to bring Meredith along next time. Gordon was so good with children; she couldn't wait to show Meredith her new daddy. A daddy that would think of mommy also. Trisha Messinal. She'd changed it back from that wop name; never believing she could love anyone as much as Gordon. Her mistake was always going for men close to her age or older. It never dawned on her that a man of twenty-four could be so mature. And he liked kids. The timing was perfect. Just as she got her life in order and she felt she could take her daughter back, he walked into her life.

It was much different than it was with Craig. Craig was a fascination to her. Cops always were. When she first saw him and his pal, Chip, in that Manhattan bar, he just stood out. His looks and demeanor just called to her. There was just something about him. She never meant to stay with him long, but he was so much fun. He was the one that didn't want to wear protection, said it didn't feel right. Of course she had to get stoned that night and forget her diaphragm, and *voila* she's a mom.

Gordon was so much better; he understood her and her needs. He wanted children with her, not just to be a parent, but also to share with her. She wasn't about to have another one, but there was no reason he couldn't adopt Meredith. It would give him the same rights and ties as a natural daughter. And once they were married, they could be one happy family.

"All set and raring to go?" Gordon called from the back of the plane.

"Ready as I'll ever be!"

The small plane whined and creaked more and more as it climbed high into the sky, leaving the south folk of Long Island far behind.

"I could see Dune Point from here. That's where my parents are." Trish laughed like a young girl.

"I hear they're just as rich as the Hamptons there," Gordon quickly added.

"That they are, even more so," Trish gladly pointed out.

"What did your dad's lawyer say this morning?" Gordon asked while checking her chute.

"Once we're married, there'll be no problem. Craig's been doing a good job of messing up his life. He leaves Meredith with a teenager every day. The lawyer said the judge is not going to like that, especially since we can both be with her twenty-four hours a day." She liked how his hands felt pulling her straps tight.

"Are you sure you want to go through with this?" he asked

"I told you, I'll jump right after you do," she responded, almost peeved.

"I meant the adoption."

"Oh, of course, I'm dying to see my little girl again," she giggled.

"You know, we can also have one of our own. I mean I still want a child that will be part of both of us."

"Meredith will be part of us, trust me. My father can make almost anything happen."

Making sure that his own chute was secure, Gordon walked to the open door of the plane.

"Are you all set, dear?"

"I'm all set," she answered.

Gordon smiled and jumped. Three seconds later, Trish followed.

It was crystal clear outside as Gordon floated down. From his view he could see the Manhattan skyline clear as a bell. He could see smoke from a brushfire somewhere near the middle of the island.

God, what a view, he thought to himself. He always loved moments like this. The idea of having a daughter in a week or so was beginning to not sound so bad. He'd have to get Trish off the pill though. That was not going to be easy. Maybe real motherhood would get her to clean up her act. Then again, if she were drugged up, he figured he could still play the field a bit. He wouldn't do it in front of the kid though. Have to watch where you dip the stick with a kid in tow. He knew his father-in-law-to-be would not like having his only grandchild talk about all the "aunts" that came over.

Ah, worry about it then.

Almost half way down, a large shadow passed over him. A moment later, a strong gust of wind took hold of the chute. It only lasted a second then disappeared. He braced himself for another one, but it never came. He tried to look up to see if a cloud had passed over, but the canopy of the parachute prevented him from seeing anything above him. The round hole on top was a perfect circle of pure blue. To his side, he could see the plane landing on the strip already. Since there were no reports of major air movement, Gordon saw no reason to worry.

The landing was perfect, as usual, and just a few feet to the right of the mark. He looked up expecting to see Trish right behind him. She was nowhere to be found. He looked around the field and only saw the pilot walking over to him from the plane.

He looked back up, only to see the clear blue sky and nothing else.

•

"What do you mean you didn't want him locked up?" Rodham stormed. "That's where you keep people in protective custody!"

"I know, but I felt he wasn't safe in our custody," Craig responded.

It was 1:30 when he got back to the squad room. He actually thought he might get away with not explaining himself. In the past, when he managed to piss Rodham off, he'd be up his ass as soon as he walked in. This time he waited, and this time he looked as if could literally explode. Craig swore he could see the man's head actually expanding.

"In my office!" is all he said in the squad room. That meant it must be embarrassing to him as well and he didn't want people to hear. Craig was going to have to muster all his charm to smooth this one out.

"What type of shit is that?" he shouted at Craig.

"The truth is, I just don't trust some of the people here. The Gercios would pay big bucks to make sure Petey never talked," Craig calmly explained.

"Bullshit! We might have some assholes here, but none of them, and I mean *none* of them, would ever turn on us!" he screamed.

So much for privacy.

"And if you did suspect anyone, why didn't you come to me?"

He was right. Despite all the politicking and manipulation Rodham was known for, he could always be trusted.

"You involve two rookies and the other two, but you don't tell me! Who do you think you are? Who gave you the balls to do a maneuver like that?"

"I'm sorry, sir. I felt the less you knew, the better. Now you can blame it all on me and come out unscathed."

"Unscathed is one way of putting it, as it seems nobody in power noticed. I only found out from others! I managed to cover your lucky ass in case people begin to look. But if they look hard, we're all fucked."

"You mean the commissioner and mayor have no idea?"

"For now, let's hope it stays that way. Meanwhile, if you ever have any doubts about any of us, I want to know," Rodham scolded. "Now who don't you trust?"

"Devaney. In all seriousness, I feel he'd kill Aisha and me if he had the chance."

"He's an asshole, don't piss in your pants over him."

"He's an asshole with a gun."

"Every department has an Devaney..."

The phone rang in the middle of Rodham's usual speech that everyone has differences. Craig heard it eight years earlier when Devaney was stupid enough to actually start a fight at Flannery's. For some reason Devaney got it into his head that Craig would be a wuss when it came to fighting. Nine years of Kempo Tai-Jitsu proved him wrong.

"Rodham here."

Immediately Craig perceived a bad vibe from his boss. The man's whole face began to lose its anger to something more chilling. Maybe the commissioner did see the news last night. Maybe the mayor did, too, and was out for blood.

"Yes, he's right here."

Shit, that's not good.

"We'll take care of him," Rodham said, then looked to Craig.

"Am I getting the ax or what?" he asked, expecting the worse. It was going too well.

"It's your ex. There's been an accident."

•

"There you are?" Jeannine yelled out when she saw Meredith again. "I was getting worried!"

"I wanted to see them catch a blowfish," Meredith said, walking back from the dock. "We had a party at camp and got out early. Are you mad at me?"

Jeannine stood over the girl crossing her arms.

"I should be! You know you're not to wander off!" With that, she reached down and started to tickle her. "I'm just gonna have to punish you with tickles."

Meredith immediately doubled over and began to laugh.

"Stop it or I'll tell Daddy you lost me."

Jeannine stopped at once. "Oh, want to play hardball, huh?"

"Yeah, what's hardball?"

"It means playing rough," she said, putting her face to Meredith's.

Just then, a cold breeze blew across their skin. At first Meredith thought that the cold grasp was coming back for her.

"Brrrr, it got chilly," Jeannine said with a shiver.

Meredith threw her arms around her in a tight grasp.

"What's this?" Jeannine asked completely surprised.

"She's back. She's back, and she wants me."

•

So much had happened since he'd left the house the night before. Craig half expected to find the house a pile of smoldering ashes by the time he got home. Mrs. McIlvain wasn't answering the phone. Not that it would have done any good. He knew that Jeannine was with Meredith down at the beach, and there would be no way to get hold of them, at least without making a scene.

How am I going to tell her that her mother is dead?

She doesn't even remember her. Will she even be upset? What about her parents? They're a pair of SOB's, but they did just lose a daughter.

And where did the body land? God, he hoped she didn't land on somebody's roof, only to be found when the people came home from work. Imagine finding the mother of his daughter had dropped in on strangers. He wanted to go to the accident site, yet he didn't want a stranger telling Meredith her mother was splattered all over the Hamptons. He remembered how the news was broken at some of the accident scenes when he was in uniform.

"Hey lady, your daughter just took a nose dive off a roof!" or "You better get down here! His head's blown off."

He remembered how some of his cohorts handled things, himself included. He knew it was wrong to say things that way, but everyone else did it, and he went along with it. It was making light of a bad situation; he used to fool himself. If he took all situations seriously, he'd go crazy.

No, it was wrong, plain and simple. Now he regretted all those times he was cold to people in tragedy and prayed it didn't happen to his daughter.

A thought entered his mind: Maybe she disappeared into thin air! Gercio disappeared into thin air! Head spinning, Craig pulled over to the side of the road. One by one the cars whizzed past him, causing the car to rock, as if he was going to be grabbed and pulled along with each one of them.

What are the odds? They both disappeared mysteriously in a matter of days of each other. Both had been threatening to him.

This isn't happening! This isn't happening!

He closed his eyes and thought of the dead cat on the side of the road and the seagull trying to fly off with it.

You are *going crazy.*

Nausea swelled in his gut. Not wanting to puke out the driver's side for all the world to see, he stretched across the passenger seat and popped the door open. Immediately, exhaust fumes and traffic noise overwhelmed him. The chili-cheese dogs had now come to life and wanted out.

I'm getting worried about you, Aisha's voice spoke in his head.

Looking down at the passenger's seat, Craig was face to face with the dragon on the book cover again.

Walk away, Albequrk's Turkish voice droned.

A whiff of fresh air filled the car. The dogs in his stomach seemed to have settled down a bit. The good feelings he had in the morning seemed to have come back.

It will be okay. Trust me, a voice called from the depth of his memory.

Craig reached forward and slammed the car door shut.

Christina Lee. The name was before his eyes again. Craig decided to give Miss Lee a call as soon as he got the chance.

•

It was 2:30 by the time Devaney called Trent Gold. He usually called him earlier before he went out on assignment, but with everything going on, he could only break free at after lunch. Good ol' Mr. Gold was going to love this one. If the dumb fuck had only gotten to the alley when he was told to, he could have scooped Scalici's group red-handed. The odds of another Scalici fuckup were slim to none, but now his wife dying mysteriously just as she was fighting for custody of their kid was sweet. Even though he knew dickhead had nothing to do with it, it would make his life miserable none-the-less. And who knows, maybe he *did* have something to do with it?

This Gold fellow obviously hated Scalici as much as he did. He was surprised to actually get Trent on the phone; he usually went through eight different people first. He always used the name Mr. Barney so nobody but Gold would know it was him.

"Trent, my good man, I have another one for ya. A real beaut."

"Does it have to do with Scalici?" he answered in an eager voice. This surprised him since Craig made him look like a blithering idiot the night before.

"Why yes, yes it does," Devaney said, having his own detective reflexes kick in. "Didn't think you'd be this eager though?"

"Damn straight I'm eager! Hope it's strange."

"As a matter a fact it is."

"Do tell. With what you told me, I'm editing together a masterpiece."

"It better not involve me!"

"Would I do that?"

"Yes."

"Smart man, what do you have?"

"His ex-wife just had an unfortunate accident."

"So, that may give him sympathy. I want to roast his nuts off."

"She was suing him for custody of their daughter. Anybody that knows him knows that he'd kill for that kid."

"Could he have been involved?"

"Hell no. She was parachuting at the east end of the island. Never made it to the ground. The chute was found, but she never landed."

"What? Oh, that's perfect! It will fit perfectly with what I'm doing."

"And what's that?"

"You'll see."

•

The early ferry back to Bay Shore was the Fire Island Belle. This made Meredith feel a little better. She grew to hate the old Queen. Not saying much to Jeannine, she sat quietly holding Jeannine's hand.

"Honey, you have to tell me what's wrong." Jeannine knew she wasn't going to get an answer. "Are you afraid of your mother? I know this is all of a sudden."

"I just want to get home," she said, and then sealed her lips.

"Is there anything you want to tell me?" Jeannine asked, dreading a response.

"There are a lot of evil people out there. I don't think Daddy can keep them away much longer," Meredith said in a blank, adult tone.

Jeannine's alarms went up. There was something that was terrifying to Meredith, something probably imaginary, but very real to her. To pry it out would only make it worse. Time to play 'Trick the Kid.'

"Since we're getting back early, why don't we get some Friendly's?" It was her favorite ice cream. "There's this new flavor ice cream, Charlie's Chocolate Cake. It's chocolate with chunks of cake in it."

"No. I want to get home."

"It's a limited flavor, they won't serve it ever again after Labor Day. What do ya say?" Jeannine prompted. She could see Meredith's face begin to change.

"Well, okay, but then we go right home," Meredith insisted.

"By your command, kid."

•

The yard was quiet and unmoving as Craig pulled into the driveway. He'd made it home again. This time, though, he didn't feel the immediate warmth that he usually did. No one was home. He never got home this early. Even in the dead of winter, he'd always see Mrs. McIlvain's light on in her room, a sign that there was life in the house. Now there was none. It was probably a senior citizens day. Although, he really did want to get home before everyone else. Nevertheless, the empty feeling from the home was palpably disturbing.

Get used to it, old boy, he told himself. *This is your life in ten years.*

"Mrs. M!" he called out from the porch, knowing there'd be no response.

How am I going to tell her? He thought, still debating on how to break the news. Will she be upset? Would she want to speak to her grandparents? How could so much be happening at once?

Unlocking the front door, something gray caught the corner of his eye. A gray Ford LTD was now parked across from the house and the two men inside were *not* cops. He also knew they were not there when he pulled in, so that meant he was followed.

Those fuckers!

Craig marched right across the lawn to their car. He could see them nonchalantly start to turn the ignition

Oh no, you don't! He thought, intending to get to them before they could pull out. As if the car heard him, the engine failed to turn over. The two men inside the car seemed to take it in stride and rolled down the window.

Without thinking, Craig pulled his revolver and placed it right up the first goon's nose. Again they seemed to take it in stride as the overpowering smell of aftershave hit Craig in the face. Both were typical mob soldiers in uniform, designer silk shirts and gold chains.

"Who the fuck are you and why are you here?" Craig smiled in his very convincing "I'm a psycho" voice.

"Whoa, Scalici, hold on. We're just out for a drive," the first goon said, trying to play it cool as the other kept a close eye on Craig's gun.

"And I'm going to shoot you if you don't tell me right now who sent you." Craig repeated shoving the barrel up the guy's nostril. "Now I don't mind cleaning the snot off my gun, but blood and brain is a bitch to get out of my clothes. Did Marcella send you?"

"No," the first goon answered short and sweet. He knew Craig had every intention of pulling the trigger.

"Good, see how easy that was? Let's see if you can do this again? Now who do you work for?"

The goon hesitated and Craig pushed the gun further.

"Palumbo!" he blurted out.

"Excellent! Now why would Palumbo be following little ol' me?"

"I don't know."

"Wrong answer." Craig cocked the gun.

"We were told to follow you after his meeting with Marcella this morning."

"You mean your boss is friendly with Sister Mary Elephant now?"

Again the man didn't speak, but nodded his head instead.

"Well dip me in shit and call me stinky! How do you like that?" Craig laughed and pulled his gun back.

"Buddy," the goon replied, "some words of advice. Get away from Marcella. The only reason we're here is because she's scarier than you! We don't bother cops."

"Oh, that's so noble of you."

"We *paisons* have to stick together."

"Just because our grandparents are from the same country does not mean we 'stick together.' My grandmother spat on scum like you! Ever come near my home again, I'll shoot you right in the head."

The goon turned the key again and this time the car magically started. Before Craig could say another word, the car was halfway down the block. He looked around and saw that none of the neighbors were looking. Not one curtain was drawn. *Thank God!*

It was then that it dawned on him, in his one hand was the revolver he had drawn, and in the other he was still holding the dragon book. He had carried it out of the car and subconsciously held onto it. Before he holstered his gun, he looked at the eyes of the dragon and the author's name Christina Lee once again.

•

Seated in their booth, Meredith polished off the last of her Charlie's Chocolate Cake Sundae. Just as Jeannine had promised, it was delicious.

She barely had enough room to finish her Fribble.

"How can a little girl like you eat so much?" Jeannine asked, finishing off her own treat.

"When it's good, I always have extra space," Meredith replied, no longer showing signs of alarm.

"That's what I say, too! Mom gets *sooo* pissed when I say that."

"Have you ever been scared of your mom? She seems scary." Meredith slurped the shallow remains of her chocolate Fribble.

"When she's mad at me, yeah?" Jeannine replied, hoping to get in the kid's head a bit. "But she'd never hurt me. She feels the same about Grandma. Grandma can be mean if she wants, but she'd never harm mom or me. Does your mother scare you?"

"How could she scare me? I've never seen her," Meredith responded in the same adult-like manner as before.

"Well, she might want to take you away from your dad." Jeannine hoped she didn't repeat what she said to Craig.

"No, Daddy won't let her."

"Then who was after you? You said a lady was after you back at the beach," Jeannine pressed, feeling her manipulation wasn't going as planned.

"Oh, the dock lady. Some of the kids in camp put some live bait in her thermos," Meredith said as she licked her sundae dish.

"Meredith! You're lying to me! You were scared to death back at the beach."

"Have you ever seen the dock lady?"

"Meredith, this isn't funny! If you don't tell me, I'm not going to take you back to the beach anymore."

"Summer's over, I don't want to go back anyway."

"Then I'll tell your father that someone is chasing you, and you won't tell me who it is."

"No, he'll think I'm a baby."

"Why would he think that?"

"Because she's not real. She's only a nightmare."

"Nightmare? What type of nightmare?"

"The type you have when you're half asleep and half awake. She tries

80

to find me, but she has trouble. She tries to look for Daddy too, but she can't see him."

"What does she look like? Do I know her?"

"I don't know what she looks like. All I know it that she's cold and mean," Meredith confessed, pushing the dish away.

Is that what happened on the Queen, did you start to fall asleep and have a nightmare?"

Meredith shook her head.

"Then what happened?"

"She's getting stronger. I don't have to be half asleep anymore. But she still has trouble finding me. Can we go home now?"

"Sure kid, let's go home."

Chapter 6

RHEA & CHRISTINA

Nine minutes after Palumbo's goons left, Jeannine came home with Meredith. Craig knew something was up for the teen beach goddess to be home before the last ferry. She simply explained that Meredith wasn't feeling well, so they came off early. This was an obvious lie from the chocolaty evidence around both their mouths.

Craig called the squad room and told Aisha and Rodham about his visitors. Again they insisted that he take a few days off, which was probably prompted by Aisha.

The big moment with Meredith came and went. She cried at first, and then went to her room. No explosive outbursts. Thank God, Trish was a bad mother. With that deed out of the way, Craig still had another one, Trish's parents. He had called them before on other occasions. He always made Meredith call and thank them for gifts. On holidays, he would always drop her off in hopes that Trish would actually play the mother role. That never happened, and in the back of his mind he knew it would never happen. Now he wondered if he should call or not. Trish was their only child, and no matter what she was like, they would be devastated. They were probably having a lot to deal with anyway. But then again, he was their son-in-law and father to their only grandchild.

Augh!

Craig knew the beach house number and the Park Avenue number. Since Thornton's retirement, it was the beach house they called home until Thanksgiving. Without wanting to agonize any more, he picked up the phone and dialed without thinking.

"Messinal residence," Hanna's German voice answered.

"Hello, Hanna it's me. How are things going over there?" Craig asked the Messinal faithful servant.

"Oh, it's not good! Mrs. Messinal is demanding a search party for Miss Trisha," Hanna explained. He could hear her cover the phone.

"They haven't found her yet?"

"Oh no! They found the parachute, but they can't find her."

"Who the hell is it, Hanna?" Thornton Messinal called out from the back.

"It's Mr. Scalici, sir," Craig heard Hanna reply. *This should be interesting.*

Thornton's ego and his clashed many a time. Craig was always very happy that old Thor was never his boss. Control of a situation was TM's credo, one of the reasons Trish turned out like she did.

"Craig! Have you heard anything?" Thornton wasted no time.

"Um, no. I don't think I'd be the one they would contact."

"Well, they're not telling us anything," he bellowed. "What's going on? Hanna said they haven't found the body."

"Not only that, the parachute was cut!"

"What? Someone cut the ropes?"

"They're not saying that. But how the hell else could it land without her? How's Sandra holding up?"

"We have her medicated! She can't even talk right now. Did you tell Meredith?" he asked in a different tone.

"Just a little while ago. I think she's in shock." He really didn't

think that, but knew it sounded good. "She asked how you two were."
She didn't.

"Oh shit. This is a nightmare!" Thornton sighed.

Tell me a bout it, Craig thought while resisting a chuckle.

"Can you talk to this creep she was with?" Thornton asked.

Craig remembered that Trish told him about someone named
Gordon. "You mean Gordon?"

"Yeah, what ever the little prick's name is."

"Um, that might not be a good idea."

"Then get one of your buddies to do it! He must have had something to do with it."

"I'll see what I can do," Craig lied.

"I'll let you know if I hear anything further. By the way, I've been
seeing you on the news a lot. Is my granddaughter safe?" Thornton suddenly asked.

"I wouldn't let a thing happen to her," he answered, resisting a snide
comment.

"That's not what I asked," Boss Messinal reminded him.

Biting his tongue, he said, "Yes, she's *very* safe."

"She better be, she's all that I have now."

"She's all that I have, too."

"I'll call you tomorrow," Thornton snapped, then hung up.

Yes! It's over with, Craig rejoiced. But he knew he'd have to deal with
it again, all too soon.

After checking on a sleeping Meredith, Craig checked the street outside. The only parked car in sight was the green Chevy. He turned back
to the house to see Julie Snow standing on the porch.

"Jeannine told me what happened. How's Meredith?" she asked.

"Fine, she didn't know the woman, but it's still traumatic."

"I don't know how important this is, but Jeannine tells me Meredith's been having nightmares about a woman coming to get her. She
seemed very frightened the past two days."

"Oh? Is it a woman she knows?" Something sparked in his head, but
he couldn't put a finger on it.

"No. At least she's not saying."

Nightmares were something Meredith hadn't had in years. The last was two years ago when she had an ear infection. "That's odd. Maybe this whole thing with her mother has her worried. By the way—don't you just love 'by the ways'?"

"Story of my life, sweetheart."

"Anyway, there might be people snooping around here. I don't think they'll do anything. But if—"

"Don't worry about me. Mother and I can dial 911 faster than anyone. Sorry she wasn't here. Her group went up to Sagamore Hill. You know, Teddy Roosevelt's place."

"Well, bully for her," he quipped. "Just be careful."

•

Remarkably, the phone remained silent for the rest of the night. Meredith came out of her room once to eat some of the pork chop Craig made for her. She didn't finish it, but he was not about to force it on her. She watched her usual 'I Dream of Jeannie' rerun and then went back to bed.

Quiet.

Again his world was quiet, but a living quiet. With his daughter in her bed, and the family upstairs, it was a quietness filled with life. He relaxed in his chair with a beer. He didn't like drinking in front of Meredith; it wasn't a good example. Since there was nothing but crap on TV, the new book seemed quite inviting. Looking at the dragon on the cover, its full beauty beckoned to him to open and read. Its colors and soft flowing lines aroused him in a way that he hadn't known for awhile. Its mouth was open in a seductive pink triangle.

He opened the cover and heard that little crack when you open a book for the first time. In its artful script, a table of stories opened up before him. A scent wafted out of the pages and tingled his nose. Going down the page, the third story's title caught his attention, "The Flight of the Dragon Rhea."

He read:

In a land once called The Old Orient, dragons were the keepers of all that was holy in nature. For thousands and thousands of years, their numbers had stayed the same. There always was, and always will be only twenty-four of them. The land and sea could only give food for that many.

One of the dragons was Rhea, the youngest. Being the river dragon, she controlled the flow of water that gave growth and life to the land. This was one of the most respected of all the dragon's charges. Upon her hundredth birthday, The Dragon Kwain, one of the mountain dragons, courted her. Rhea fell deeply under Kwain's spell. Her mother, the Dragon Chi, instructed her never to see Kwain, for she was too young to take a mate, and dragons only mated when one has died. But Rhea did not listen to her mother.

Kwain's charm was strong and inviting. She used to meet with him when the tide was low and listen to his tales of battle and conquest. Then one night when the moon was red in the sky, Rhea succumbed to Kwain's courtship and took him as her mate. From this, six eggs swelled deep in Rhea's body. This was forbidden, for there could only be the number twenty-four. It was therefore decreed that Rhea must devour all her eggs once they were laid. Rhea did not want to kill her young, and pleaded with the elders to let her keep the children. She even offered to sacrifice herself to provide more food for them. Alas, they did not listen.

So on the coldest night of the year, Rhea flooded the plains with all of the rivers in the land. The rivers quickly froze, creating vast wastelands that became swamps in the spring. Some say it was her tears in the water that became the rice crops of the next harvest season. As the other dragons tried to drain the water, Rhea flew away to the west where the sun would set.

She flew many, many days, past far away lands that the other dragons had never seen. Finally she came to a great ocean. With her eggs ready to be laid, she made a nest high in the mountains. From the eggs hatched two sons and four daughters. Each one was greatly different from the other, and all were much different than their ancestors in the old land.

Craig scanned ahead, the story then started to talk about the different children and the children they had. He flipped through the book, then to the author's page in the back. A small black and white photo showed Christina Lee. She had her head tilted onto her hand, letting her long black hair hang down like a silk drape. Her almond shaped eyes met his as if she were there in-person. Her round face framed a supple smile as if she were about to start laughing at the photographer for being too serious. Underneath was a small bio:

Dr. Christina Lee is the department chair for Asian/European Folklore at C. W. Post College in Greenville, New York.

My, she looks awfully young to be a professor, he thought. He closed the book and thought of what an asshole The Dragon Kwain was for abandoning his wife and kids. Why did so many old stories portray fathers as heartless bastards? For a moment Craig thought of his own dad who had died when Craig was just eighteen. He remembered that he felt nothing for the man, neither love nor hatred. The man was a non-entity to him. If it weren't for his mother dying when he was born, Craig felt his dad would have left him long before that.

Then he thought of Thornton and how he treated Trisha. To him, Trisha was employed as his daughter. And due to the union, he could not fire her for bad job performance.

What is with these people? He thought. *Are they really that selfish?*

Again, Craig was able to put the day's woes away for a while. As long as Meredith was healthy and safe, all else seemed unimportant.

•

In his dreams, Craig took flight again, this time without the benefit of a dragon. He could see the lights of the South Shore below him. In a group of lights on the grounds, he recognized the campus of C. W. Post College. He had gone to a seminar there once on serial killers. Before he knew it, he was standing naked in front of the wrought iron gates at the entrance. There was no one to be seen. All the lights were lit in the parking lot, but not a living soul around.

He slowly walked toward the buildings, yet managed to get there in a blink of an eye. One light was lit on the third floor. Craig felt his manhood below throb and stir as he waited for Christina to appear in the window. She did. Craig's penis was now fully erect as Christina looked down to him. Instead of being embarrassed as he usually did in these dreams, Craig stood there for her to see him.

"Who are you?" she asked with that smile from the book.

"Detective Scalici. I'm here to question you." He felt his body tingling. "Will you answer my questions?"

She smiled, "Yes."

•

Craig woke up to find a wet dream finalizing in his pants.

"Shit!" escaped his lips as he spilled the beer still in his hand. It landed right in his lap creating more of a mess.

"SHIT!"

He tried to cup it so it wouldn't seep into the chair, creating a pool in his crotch. Slowly, his pants absorbed the mess sparing the chair.

That's what I get for drinking and sitting.

He waddled to the bathroom and removed all his clothes. Evil flashbacks to adolescence came back while he piled his skivvies on the spotless tile floor.

It's cold in here.

He felt a chill wrap around his leg, then his penis. To his surprise, he felt himself get mad.

Get out of here! raced through his mind. Immediately the chill was gone.

•

The phone rang the next morning. It was Sandra Messinal.

"Good morning, Craig," she spoke in a groggy, but sober tone.

"Morning, Sandra, how are you holding up?" Craig asked feeling awkward as hell. He still remembered the time she referred to him as greasy Italian trash when she thought he was out of earshot.

Thanks for the memory, Sandra.

"I'm still here. They haven't found her yet. Did you hear anything?" she asked with a forced composure.

"Um, no." He didn't want to admit he didn't do a thing.

"I was wondering if we could have Meredith for the day?" she asked.

"I don't know if that's a good idea. Maybe when things calm down," he said, trying to be as diplomatic as possible.

"Things are pretty calm now. We can't make plans without the body, even if she's dead. And it will free you up to talk to the police."

He didn't have the heart to tell her that there was nothing he could do. One lesson he learned was to keep his nose out of another cops' work. The last thing the investigating officer wants to see is a victim's cop ex-husband interfering. Then again, there were similarities between Gercio and Trish. God forbid they find Trish the same way they found Gercio.

"I'll see what I can do," finally came from his mouth. "As for Meredith..."

"I want to go, Daddy." Meredith's voice spoke up behind him. She seemed unusually quiet, almost mature beyond her years.

"Honey, things are going to be hectic over there," he explained, making sure the phone was covered.

"They need me, Daddy. Who else do they have?" she asked, with more clarity than her grandmother on the line.

Craig knew it was wrong, every cell in his body told him so. Yet his brain told him there was no reason not to. Thoughts of them taking her and flying off to Europe with her filled his head.

That's paranoia, Craiger. His mind told him. That's a symptom of going bonkers.

Craig looked to Meredith's eyes and knew that he had nothing to worry about.

"Yes Sandra, I'll put her on the next boat," he answered.

"Thank you. And you don't have to worry about anybody blubbering in front of her. My pills have seen to that," she said in rare display of candor.

"You're welcome. And Sandra, I'm truly sorry this had to happen." The fact was, he was only sorry about Meredith not ever having a mother, and that they had to deal with the loss of a daughter. But as far as Trish was concerned, he was indifferent. Like his dad, he couldn't care less about her.

•

It was Mrs. McIlvain that came to the door. He always knew when she was home alone; it always took a few minutes to get to the door.

"Morning, Mom," Craig greeted her.

"Why, good morning, Detective. How are you holding up?" she asked with her usual smile.

"As well could be expected. I just wanted to let you know that I'm sending Meredith to her grandparents for the day," he said, realizing how much more of a grandmother Mrs. McIlvain had been instead of Sandra.

"I'll let Jeannine know. She was quite worried about her."

"In case you have any unexpected visitors while I'm gone, you shouldn't let them in the house."

"I may be old, but I know better. Don't you fret over me, for cripes sake," she said, waving her finger. "You watch out for yourself. You're too handsome to get shot or worse."

"Don't you fret over me either." He winked to her as he went to fetch Meredith.

When he dropped her off at the special Dune Point Ferry, Meredith seemed happy she wasn't going to take the old Queen. She got on with no problem and waved goodbye. After the boat left, he sat behind the wheel to decide what to do. If it weren't for picking up Meredith, he'd just as soon go into work. But a day off was rare. He could look into Trish's accident, or he could go to the college to talk about dragons with Miss Lee.

Could a dragon have eaten Trish? Or maybe somebody wants it to look that way? Again, he found himself thinking about the ludicrous. Either way, he wanted to know more about dragons.

His first stop was to the fifth precinct out in Riverhead. He assumed they'd be the ones handling the case. Sure enough, there was nothing to be learned. They told him that the ropes of the parachute looked as if they were torn off the harness. If they were clean cut, then they would suspect something. In their minds, it was a freak accident and air currents to the ocean carried her body away. They were checking the flight plans though, in case she got caught in a jet engine. But that was a shot in the dark.

With that out of the way, he drove to the other end of Long Island to the campus of C. W. Post.

As in his dream, which he had full memory of, the gates stood exactly the same. He drove his Mustang through the parking lot, feeling like he was a college geek again. He, himself, only lasted two months at Suffolk Community. When his dad quit living, he quit college.

At the end of the lot, the brick building that he knew was hers stood with dozens of coeds piling out. Thinking back, he remembered an ex-girlfriend named Michele had gone to Post. He wondered whatever became of many of his friends from childhood. He seemed to have lost touch with them all. In the lobby of the building, he heard the voices of all the new members of adulthood. What a breath of fresh air it was to hear people talk about plans and life. At the police station, or any other work place, people griped about anything just to complain. God knows you always had to complain about something.

He looked for Professor Lee on the black pegboard directory. Sure enough, there she was under Asian/European Studies in plastic white letters. Eerily, she was located in room 303.

The third floor, just like my dream.

As he made his way up the steps, the crowd of students began to thin out as the next hour of classes approached. By the time he made it to the third floor, the halls were empty. All the doors were closed except the third one down. Sunlight beamed through it into the hallway from an open window.

303, no doubt.

When he walked into the office, he saw Christina Lee. Unlike his dream, she was wearing thick glasses with black rims. The long hair he had expected was tied in a bun, and she was dressed in a frumpy gray suit. Standing on a chair, she was watering a spider plant hanging from the ceiling and completely unaware of his entrance. Despite her appearance, he could tell she was definitely a beautiful woman.

"Dr. Lee?" he asked.

"In a minute," she said in a tone means for students in and out of the office all day. "Herman needs his water."

She finished watering and finally looked down to Craig and gasped. The water bottle fell out of her hands and Craig grabbed it before it hit the ground. Unfortunately, half the water splashed back up and the wave of water hit him right in the crotch.

"Oh, I'm so sorry," she cried.

"It's okay, I'm getting used to it," he joked.

"Aren't you Detective Scalici, from TV?" she asked, stepping down.

"Actually, I'm his evil twin, Louie."

"Well, evil twin Louie, what brings you here?" she asked, retrieving her water bottle.

"Unofficial police business," he said, looking at the mess in his lap.

A genuine look of concern filled her eyes as he saw them widen behind the glasses. "Oh, I hope it's not one of my students?"

"No actually, I'm here about your dragon book."

Now the concern turned to surprise. While standing in the office, he explained that he felt there were a group of people murdering gangsters and making look as if a dragon was doing it. He didn't mention Trish.

"Detective, I don't know how I could help you. There is no single folklore about dragons. Every culture seems to have them. They do usually stand for something else, though. Back when people couldn't openly speak bad of a ruling body, they used dragon tales as metaphors."

"Like the story of Rhea?" he asked her, thinking of the response it provoked in him the night before.

"Good example. The story of Rhea talks not only about the mistreatment of women, but how society doesn't look beyond its borders. Are you an intellect, Detective?"

"No, I'm a Leo," he smiled.

"I see your wit is just as quick off the screen as on."

"You make it sound as if I'm a TV star."

"You are! I saw you with Trent Gold, Live Action News," she deepened her voice to imitate Trent. "I even saw it when that mob boss threatened you."

"Isn't that a perk of the trade? To have beautiful women wanting my autograph?"

"That's why I was so shocked when I saw you," she said, secretly thinking of her own vivid dream she had of him the night before.

"What else can you tell me about dragons that may be of help?" he asked, still feeling the water running down his legs.

She looked at her watch, then at his pants.

"Hum, I only have an hour 'til my next lecture. Why don't you change into some sweats I have and join me for lunch? The dining hall is *tres magnifique*. I'll even buy. The weenies and mustard are on me. You've had enough on you today."

•

Mrs. McIlvain sat on her porch watching the summer's day go by. She had seen so many of them in her years and never tired of just being a part of it. It was nicer when the little girl was home and playing outside. It wasn't a complete summer unless children were playing. There were a few times when she wanted to get up and join her, but she knew better.

Once in a while she saw a gray LTD drive past the house. The last time she actually waved to them. Around 11:00 AM, a cream-colored sports car pulled up. It had one of those snotty Germany symbols on the front. A young man around the same age as the Detective got out and looked around as if he were pressed for time. There was nothing about him to warrant a call to the police. He looked all of 150 pounds and stood six-one with gold-rimmed glasses. From her seat, with the help of her own glasses, she could see a gold Star of David around his neck.

"Good morning, ma'am," the young man greeted her, walking up to the porch, but keeping a respectful distance.

"If you are looking for detective Scalici, he's not home," she informed him nicely, still keeping a watchful eye on his distance. By the way his head lowered, she could tell she had confirmed something he didn't want to hear.

"That's too bad," he replied, disappointed.

"What's your name, young man?" she asked, seeming to surprise him.

"I'm sorry ma'am?" he replied, not expecting the question.

"Your name. It is polite to leave your name in a situation such as this."

"Um, Tim. I'll try again later. By any chance, can you give me his phone number? I know it's unlisted, but it's important that I talk to him." He looked as if he was on the verge of desperation.

"I'm sorry, young fella, I think you know I can't. If you want, I'll leave a message for him."

"No. I'd rather check back later," he replied.

"Are you all right, young Tim? You seem nervous."

"I have to go. Please forget I was even here."

She watched him drive off in a hurry. Moments later the LTD drove by again, and again she waved. A half hour later a brown van pulled up front. From the back, a man got out with a TV camera and started filming the house. She waved to them too. After a minute, they packed up and left. And for the rest of the day, Grandma M sat there enjoying the summer day.

•

"They're said to be xenomorphic," Christina added.

"Say what?" was Craig's reply as they sat in the dining hall. Craig felt stupid as hell sitting there. He thought he gave the appearance of a student's father trying too hard to be 'one' with his college son. Along with the sweats, all he needed was a baseball cap that read 'I Tappa Keg' or something to that effect. Besides, he had no idea what xenomorphic meant.

"They can change forms. Take on the appearance of any animal or man," she giggled.

"And what's so funny?" he asked, not liking the situation one bit.

"You look more like a frat house president than a detective."

"More like his dad."

"Maybe older brother."

"So does this mean they can take human form and have children?" he asked, trying again to be professional.

"Most folklore says no, but there are a few European stories that mention mating with witches. Supposedly, the magic of dragons and witches are similar enough to allow a union," she explained, finishing off her hotdog.

"So dragons are magical?" he asked with a renewed intensity.

"According to legend, yes. But they're not really," she responded, looking at him oddly.

"Why do you say that?" He was eager for an answer.

"Because they're not real, detective."

Craig was stunned for a moment. He felt as if Christina saw right into his head. But as usual, his quick mouth saved him.

"Not to the people doing this. They have gone to great lengths to make it appear as if a dragon is murdering people.

"I agree there's a lot of sick people out there, but this would require a rather elaborate rouse."

"These people go to unimaginable lengths to set an example."

"You're talking helicopters and vats of acid."

"Then how else would you explain it, Professor?"

Christina stared back at him, then shrugged her shoulders.

"Well, if it wasn't a group of people, what else could it be?"

She looked at him in all seriousness. "Something I don't want to meet."

They sat in silence. It was unspoken, but they both knew a dragon was responsible, and neither one wanted to be the first to admit to it.

"Now about your sweats?" he asked. Christina seemed more than happy to discuss something else.

"Keep them, I get them cheap from the bookstore," she smiled, getting up and checking her watch.

"One last question. Can dragons control air temperature? Like making it cold out?"

"They're magical, Detective. And I suppose they probably could do a lot of things...if they existed."

Chapter 7

POISONED EARTH

"Poisoned earth, powdered fine, to the powdered cat I join," she chanted. "Not the worst, but yet the best, for my vengeance, for the rest. 'Tis a poison which when done, will rack and ruin many-of-one. And they shall know no good or peace, nor their suffering ever cease, until they humbly come to me, and beg for mercy on their knees. Which I may grant, if I should please."

The spell was cast.

•

Lou Terrell called in all his favors and managed to get Gercio's remains released to Marcella. He felt this would be the perfect time to act. She was no idiot, and this would be the only time he could take her out. Staying at his office downtown was the safest place. Unlike the depictions on TV, he controlled things from a regular office building instead of an Italian restaurant. Once, as a joke on the Feds, he wanted to set up shop at a doughnut shop, just to get feedback on what he said. For the most part, though, business was run from the 30th floor. In the worst case scenario, he had a helicopter prepped on the roof at all times.

As soon as he knew Marcella was heading to the funeral home to select a casket, he would pick up the phone to order the hit. His heart pounded hard. He had made similar calls before, but Marcella scared him like no other. Her eyes were beyond dark brown—they were black. With a trembling hand, he started to dial. Knowing the number by heart, he dialed it, then pressed the wrong number at the end. He dialed again, his pulse growing heavier in his head. Again he got to the end and hit the wrong number.

"Fuck," he said to himself in frustration. He dialed again, got to the last number and missed. "Come on, you fuck!"

Meow. Came from ahead of him.

He looked up, and on the floor sat a black cat.

Meooow, came from its mouth, as if someone were speaking it through a microphone.

Old Louie stopped cold and looked at the animal's green eyes. Their black slit pupils bore down on him. The cat stood and arched its back. Its hair stood on end as it spat at him.

From his drawer, he pulled the Saturday Night Special he'd never had to use. He brought it up, then all the buttons on the phone pressed down at once. The chorus of tones rung out and his attention diverted to the receiver for a second.

The cat had jumped on the desk. The stench of dead, rotted fish overwhelmed him as the cat swiped its paw at his neck.

Lou felt no pain, just the sharp tug on his windpipe. If he had been looking in the mirror, he would have seen his entire Adam's apple was now a gaping hole. Hissing, the cat jumped and shoved its way into the wound. Powerless, he could feel it clawing its way further in.

Again, the stench of rotted fish overtook him, more than the actual clawing to his heart. Before he died, he realized his fatal mistake.

Marcella really was a witch.

•

Before leaving the campus, Craig called the beach house. He wanted to head off Thornton before he called him. He explained what the investigators felt, and that the Coast Guard was now patrolling the coast line. After good ol' Thor proclaimed it incompetent crap, he put Meredith on the line.

"How are you doing, sweetie? How's grandma and grandpa?" He hoped she wasn't too upset.

"They're fine. Grandma and I have been reading some of mom's old storybooks. I saw your wedding picture," she exclaimed, as if she had discovered King Tut's tomb. He had a copy himself somewhere. "You two were a beautiful couple."

"Why thank you, hon. Your mother was a beautiful lady." And that was no lie.

"I was wondering if I could stay the night?" she asked.

"No."

"Why not?"

"Because I said so."

"But Hanna's going to make waffles in the morning," Meredith began to plead.

"No! Grandma and grandpa have a lot on their minds. I want you home, young lady."

"But *Daaaddy!*"

"No buts! I'll let you stay till the eight o'clock boat, but that's it. I'll pick you up then."

"Yes, sir," she reluctantly answered.

"Now don't forget to thank your grandma." He heard her turn around and do just that. Then he heard her say that she couldn't stay. He could hear Sandra pause and say, "Okay."

"Love you, dear," Craig told his daughter.

"Love you too, Daddy," she answered, then hung up.

Craig listened to the dial tone a bit, then called the station house.

"Hi, Craig," Aisha answered.

"How did you know it was me?" Craig asked, perplexed.

"How do I know my kids won't clean their rooms? It's a law of nature."

"Am I that predictable?"

"When it comes to some things, I can set my watch by you. And I'll bet you'll be in tomorrow," she added.

"I might stay home. I have the time," he said, looking at Christina's building. "And the desire."

"Not when I give you an update, sweet cheeks."

"Oh-oh, sweet cheeks means bad. Let me have it."

"One, Albequrk released Gercio's remains. Two, Louie Terrell was whacked in his office. And three, the Feds are here."

"Hum, well, in respective order…no big deal, holy shit, and I don't give a rat's ass."

"You better give one on the last answer."

"I care more about Terrell. Homicide give you any details?"

"Not yet, I just got word of it myself. Any word on Trish?"

"Nothing, literally. They feel the harness broke away from the chute and an air current landed her out at sea." He was still holding his wet clothes in a plastic bag.

"Tell me, how do you stay so cool in all of this?"

"I'm abnormal, remember? I should be stressed out, but I'm not—."

She cut him off, "You're not abnormal! That's not what I said! I just hope everything doesn't overwhelm you at once."

"And I appreciate it. I'll be in tomorrow."

"You don't have to."

"What, and miss Gercio's funeral?"

"Oh no, don't you dare!" she warned.

"What, and miss a chance to say hello to Marcella?"

"You are nuts!"

"Just call me Cashew."

"I'll be calling you corpse!" she yelled back, then popped back with something she almost forgot. "Oh, and one other thing. Someone's been calling, asking questions about Trisha."

"Probably the Suffolk guys. They're just checking up on me. I'd do the same thing."

"These weren't from a cop, more like a reporter. A couple of people told me they got calls today."

"Oh really?" Craig didn't like the sound of that at all.

"See you tomorrow, partner."

"See ya."

Without interruption, Craig drove straight home.

•

By the time Craig had pulled on to the Long Island Expressway to go home, Timothy Zimmer had made it all the way back to his estate. He thought for sure Scalici would have been home the day after his wife was murdered, and he knew she was. But he had gambled and lost. There was no way Marcella would let him out of her sights another day. She was on to him. But he felt certain she had no idea what he was up to, if she did, he'd be dead.

After the house was a no go, he went back to the temple to pick up Georgy. Like Scalici, the only thing he had in his life was his child. If Scalici only knew what was happening, he'd probably have the kid locked up at the Vatican. Marcella would never purposely hurt their child, that much he knew. But her evil had grown by leaps and bounds over the past year.

He needed the detective's help in escaping from her.

There was something about the detective that always enraged Marcella. She must be up to something, or she would have done away with Scalici by now, along with his little girl. There was no doubt in his mind that Marcella rubbed out Scalici's ex. How long would it be before he just died or mysteriously disappeared?

Georgy sat strapped into the passenger's seat playing with his little green army men. They belonged to Tim when he was young. His mother gave them to him on the first night of Chanukah 1959, something he never told his wife. A part of him wanted to be that child again, not worrying about all the shit going on now. He'd even settle on being an oblivious oaf up in the boonies.

Unfortunately, his once beautiful bride was now one of the darkest forces the world had ever known. He had seen first hand what she could do. There was still a place in her heart for him, but it was getting smaller day-by-day. Only Georgy was keeping him alive right now. It was good in the sense that she didn't want him exposed to her evil, yet. He hid the child at the synagogue where his mother once went. Marcella would not be able to see into such a sacred place and assume he was in there too.

He pulled up to the evil mansion that she called home—and he called hell.

•

"Where the hell have you been?" Marcella hollered. "You were supposed to go to the zoo!"

"And how many others knew that too!" Tim calmly replied. "You wanted us away and safe, we were away and safe."

"So where *did* you go?" she demanded, standing there with her fists embedded on her hips.

"We went to temple. I figured it was a safe place," he told her flat out, almost hoping she'd kill him on the spot.

"How fucking safe could it be if I can't see you?"

"If you can't find us, no one can!" he threw back at her. Once in a blue moon she did listen to him.

She stopped short, and looked out her attack window. His words, as usual, cut through all the other bullshit of the day. They always made perfect sense even though she could tell he was lying. She still cared too much for him to get rid of him.

"Sorry if I want to keep our son safe from your cohorts!" he piled it on, still knowing how to get to her. "Did you get what you want today?" He knew that getting her to boast about her conquest would get her to forget about his own activities. It worked like a charm.

"Perfectly. Old Lou did exactly what I expected, when I expected," she cooed.

"What spell did you use?" he asked calmly, but trembled inside.

"I sent Felix," she smiled, putting her hands on his shoulders.

"So they released Dad?" He put his arms around her in his best performance yet.

"Yes. I'm burying him tomorrow," she answered in her most seductive voice that now made Tim's skin crawl.

"You always were smarter than the rest." He caressed her cheek.

"I still have to deal with the dragon," she confided, showing a rare glimmer of doubt.

"You'll be fine," he assured her.

"I know. And honey," she kissed him lightly, "if you're fucking with me, I'll kill you."

•

"A nice Jewish boy named Tim?" Craig asked Mrs. McIlvain.

"That's what I said. And the van and the mob guys," she repeated.

"How did you know they were mob guys?"

"Mr. McIlvain used to knock their sleazy heads together on the force."

"And what about the van? Were they mob guys?"

"No, they were too white," she said to his surprise. "They looked like those college guys."

"This Tim, what did he drive?"

"One of those sports cars, looked real expensive," she explained, sipping her Tab.

"I don't know any..." Craig started to say, but then it dawned on him. "Timothy?"

She answered. "That's what Tim stands for. Is he dangerous? He didn't look it. Then again, looks are deceiving."

"He's not dangerous at all." He wondered why he had come. What could he want, unless he wanted away from Marcella? Now that her father was dead, she had no power. But maybe she did?

"When's Meredith coming home?" Mrs. McIlvain asked, as if nothing was wrong. "I baked her an apple pie. Thought she'd like to have it with some tea."

"Not until eight. Then I think it's best she get some sleep."

"Nonsense, children always like pie. If your friend had stayed around longer, I would have given him some."

"That's very sweet of you, but I really want her to get some rest."

"Then I'll just save it for the two of you."

"Thank you," he smiled. "Tell me, has there been anything else strange around here? You know I don't want anything to happen to you or your family."

"Don't worry, what could possibly happen?"

•

The eight o' clock ferry pulled in just as Craig arrived. Behind it, the sun was setting in its colorful brilliance. The daylight had waned to the point that a shadowy haze floated in the air. He could see the boat clearly, but the inside remained dark. Sitting on the hood of his car, he could see some white tee shirts floating inside the ferry with no faces visible. Meredith was nowhere on top, so he figured she had to be inside. Seagulls cried all around him as they swooped down to the water then perched on one of the pier's pylons.

Moments later, Meredith appeared out of the darkness of the ship. He could see every last detail of her as she stood by the ferry's door, waving to him. Warmth suddenly overwhelmed him to the point of tears. He hated to be sappy, but the image of his daughter at that moment drove him to tears. For Craig, there was no deeper love in his being than the love he felt for his daughter.

"Hi, Daddy," she called to him, waving her arm.

"Hi, sweetheart." He waved back, drying his tears. Had anyone asked, they were due to the salt.

As the boat pulled in, two other images appeared behind her. His heart literally stopped for a second and the blood flushed out of his face as he saw Sandra and Thornton standing behind her. They were also waving to him. Head spinning, Craig felt his body sway to the point that he thought he was going to fall right off the hood of the car. With all his gusto, he continued to smile and wave back. The ferrymen tied the boat off and Meredith was the first one off. Craig snatched her up immediately into his arms.

"And how are you? Were you good for grandma and grandpa?" he asked, staring deep into her dark blue eyes, wanting them to always be there.

"She was a pleaser." Sandra's voice reached him from far away. "She could stay with us anytime."

Still holding her, Craig looked up to see his in-laws encroaching on him.

"Well, this is a surprise." Craig held his daughter tighter.

"It was such a beautiful night, we thought we'd take the ride with her," Thornton smiled, wearing his black and white checkered pants. Sandra held his arm in slacks and a blouse, instead of the usual tennis dress.

"Why that was very nice. What do you say, dear?" he prompted Meredith.

"Thank you," she said for the fifth time, then turned to her dad. "Did they find mommy yet?"

"No, not yet." Craig answered at a complete loss on how to act.

Thornton said to Meredith, "Meredith, why don't you buckle up in your daddy's car. I want to talk to him."

"Okay." She obeyed immediately and motioned to get down from Craig's arms.

A rage consumed Craig immediately. If Meredith still wasn't in his hands, he would have belted Thor right in the face. How *dare* he tell her what to do. With all his training in marshal arts, he restrained himself for the good of the child. He put Meredith down and opened the door for her.

"Thanks, Daddy," she said, hopping in.

Restraining himself, he turned back to Trish's parents.

"How are you two doing?" he asked with a more serious tone, resisting every urge in his body. They were her only other relatives.

"I don't know," Sandra answered first. "I don't know what to feel. I think she's still alive."

"She fell out of a plane for crying out loud!" Thor snapped at her in his normal passive-aggressive way. "Of course she's dead."

Craig told them, "I've talked to the police and the coast guard. I gave them your number and they'll call you the moment they find anything."

For a long moment they all just stood there. Then Thornton finally broke the ice.

"You're looking good there, son," he complemented.

I'm not your son!

"Thanks, Thornton. You both look healthy, too." He didn't know what else to say to them.

"Thanks again for letting us have Meredith over," Sandra said. "It helped me a lot."

"I wish I could do more." Craig forced a smile of concern

"If you don't mind, we'd like to have Meredith with us more often," Thor threw it in quickly.

Craig could feel the man sizing him up for a reaction. "That's going to be hard. School starts up in a few days," Craig replied, thanking God for the Islip school system.

The couple exchanged glances.

Thornton quickly said, "Well, we've decided to live out here year round. We could still see her on the weekends."

Smiling the whole time, Craig began to lose it. "You think just because you lost one daughter, you could replace her with another! There is no way I will *ever* let you two do to Meredith what you did to Trish." He growled like an animal about to pounce.

"Now hold on," Thor replied in a soft voice. "We just want to see more of her. We don't want to take her away from you."

"I am sorry that Trish is dead," Craig said matter-of-factly.

"She's not dead!" Sandra injected. "If she were dead, they'd have found her by now."

"I don't care." Craig finally broke. "I couldn't care less. She was a lousy person, and a lousy mother. And you two made her that way."

Again they were all quiet. The whole argument was quiet.

"Now please, just let us be," he said.

Whoosh.

The sound of air rushing by flew over their head. For a moment the dark shadow of an enormous plane passed by, cutting out the remaining sun. Everyone on the dock looked up only to see the remnants of a strong breeze blowing through the trees. The timing was perfect. The in-laws were distracted long enough for Craig to back to the car. By the time they looked back down. He was already opening the car door.

"I'll let you know if I hear anything," he said, climbing behind the wheel.

Meredith stuck her head out the window she had just cracked open. "Love you, Grandma, love you, Grandpa."

Pulling out of the parking lot, Craig looked in his rearview and saw the old couple watching them leave. Sandra was in Thornton's arms crying.

•

"Oh, this is *sooo* sweet!" Trent Gold spoke out loud to himself.

Devaney had managed to get him into the crime scene where Boss Lou Terrell was mutilated. He didn't know how much of it he could get past the censors, but just the description the secretary gave of the body should be enough. Since he was doing the editing, the whole story was going to be a shocking surprise to everyone. The station's ratings were in the shit hole ever since they lost baseball. They needed something to boost the ratings, so he might be able to get the entire tape shown. They had started running the promos already, they just had to wait for them to plant Gercio in the ground and his work of art would be done. He wasn't going to get the Edward R. Murrow award for it, but he was going to get noticed. Scalici's good luck was about to evaporate.

•

Benny entered the room of the Dragon, the head of the Blood Triad. The Chinese gangs were a group that gave him the willies, almost as much as his boss. Unlike the Families, the Triads were silent. There was a cool, calculated thought behind those eyes, and nothing else. It was an honor that they even allowed him to speak. Marcella must have done something, since they never spoke to non-Asians. Most people underestimated them, thinking they ran nothing but laundries and egg roll shops. He knew better. Benny knew they were the ones that would be Marcella's biggest obstacle.

Feeling wary, he looked at the men around him. Most were nothing more then teenagers, much like he was at that age and proving his manhood. The room was dark but clear of smoke, something any TV movie of the week would provide. The Dragon himself was at the head of a Formica table that looked like it belonged in his grandmother's kitchen. A small man, with eyes looking as big as saucers behind his glass, he commanded power from everyone in his presence, including Benny. Two bodyguards, in their forties, stood on either side of him. They must have been standing there for at least twenty years, wherever the Dragon was.

The Dragon spoke perfect English. "Mr. Esposito, I must admit you have perked my interest. I trust you are not wasting my time."

"Time is money, sir. I do not believe in wasting it," Benny replied. "My boss is preoccupied at the moment, thank you for seeing me on such short notice."

"Come now, Mr. Esposito, your actions here were well planned out. You know I've been watching you and your activities. I do question your loyalties." The Dragon asked simply and businesslike, "If you turn on your own, what prevents you from turning on us?"

"You are a man of respect. My boss now has no respect for business and the way things are done. She is a woman. She may be forceful, but she does not have the ability to control things as you can." Benny hoped they wouldn't slash his throat for saying the wrong word at the wrong time.

"A very understandable rationale. Basically you think I can run her operations better than she can. I'm flattered that you hold my organization in such high regard. Unfortunately, Mr. Esposito, your businesses are way too conspicuous for us. You almost welcome notoriety. The appeal of acquiring your enterprises is luring, but unrealistic. A fact someone of your intelligence must realize."

Before he knew it, Benny felt the cold steel of a blade at his throat, as one of the kids yanked his head back by his perfect hair.

"So now I ask you, why are you here?" The Dragon asked. "You *know* we do not deal outside our own."

"I came to give you something," Benny said.

The Dragon thought this odd. They stripped him and found nothing. He had a gun in its holster, and one strapped to his ankle. His wallet held $120, and there were only his gold rings.

"If it is a message, why did you…"

"It's not a message." Benny laughed.

The Dragon noticed the necklace Benny wore around his neck. Instead of the usual gold chain, it was a leather strap with an animal head, a goat. Instinctively he knew this was not what it appeared to be. The only reason the woman would send this man was to get him close to him. He raised his hand and gave the order to slice. As the boy went to swipe, his arm froze. The Dragon saw the look in his face as his arm did not do as it was commanded.

The eyes of the goat began to glow a dull orange. Benny began to smile.

The Dragon nodded his head, giving the order to kill. Everyone in the room pulled their guns, but could not fire. The connection between their brains and trigger fingers seemed to have been disconnected.

Benny laughed even louder as the room began to change. The shadows of the men began to move on their own.

"Kill him!" The Dragon ordered, not caring for those in back of Benny.

On the walls the shadows of the men seemed to walk together to form one great shadow. Then the shadow began to change its shape. Its outline became rounder, feminine. Before his very eyes Marcella appeared before him, as if her shadow projected her physical body directly in front of him.

"I so glad to finally meet you. If you would only have agreed to meet with such an inferior woman such as myself, I would have spared the dramatics," she said, wearing a black silk gown.

"How did you get in here?" The Dragon demanded, looking around as his men struggled to pull their triggers.

"You let me in with Benny here," she said, while Benny slipped from under the frozen knife. "Oh, I also used a little bit of black magic."

"If you wish to kill me, go right ahead. The others will follow, and get their revenge in the night." The Dragon maintained his composure.

"Kill you? If I wanted you dead, Dragon, I would have killed you this morning while you ate your cantaloupe and rice cake. I can see you and kill you anytime I want. But I want you alive." She glided over to him, her hulking body moving as smooth as her silk dress.

"If you think I will give you anything, you are sadly mistaken," he informed her, still keeping his composure.

"You will do my bidding. Your kind always do." She walked around behind him.

The Dragon noticed that none of his men could move at all. Their eyes wildly darted around trying to make sense of the situation. He saw Benny walk over to his trusted guard for two decades and retrieve his guns from his waistband. He could see the guard's eyes bulge in frustration at not being able to move.

"I will die before I do anything for you," he seethed, turning around to her. She towered over the old man, glaring down.

"No, but you will wish you had."

"How do you propose to do this?" he asked, glaring up to her.

"Fear." She walked over to the guard from whom Benny had retrieved his guns. "Die." She spoke and touched the man on his shoulder. As if turning off a child's toy, the guard just fell to the ground dead.

"You cannot scare me," the old man smiled.

"Oh really?" Marcella smirked, then bent over him. She brought her eyes up to his. "They say your eyes are windows to your soul. Look into my soul old man, then tell me you are not scared."

A moment later, he was at her bidding.

•

That night Craig dreamed of Christina again.

Chapter 8

PLANTING GERCIO

The old cemetery appeared to span endlessly. A field of tombstones seemed to end at the New York City skyline itself. The spell of beautiful sunny days had ended with gray clouds overcastting the sky with a damp veil.

Craig and Aisha watch the procession of black limos and flower cars as they snaked in the narrow road of the bone-old burial ground. They sat there as all the mourners piled out of their limos and huddled around the hearse.

"My God. President Johnson didn't have this much pomp and circumstance," Aisha quipped, sipping her coffee.

"He wasn't as powerful," Craig responded.

Again Aisha worried for her partner. He was definitely obsessing.

They continued to watch as well-known actors and other socialites join the crowd. It sickened Craig that these people would surround themselves with murderers. The way they would show their "wild-side" by chumming around with people who shot their best childhood pal in the back of the head without a second thought. Yet none of them got close to Marcella. They must have sensed she was too evil to be a good photo op.

Gercio's casket was spectacular. As it was pulled from the back of the hearse, its gold trim gleamed like a campfire. Marcella stood to the side, clutching her son's hand and actually showing genuine grief. Craig immediately remembered his own dad's burial. He remembered how he felt nothing, nothing at all.

"What's wrong?" Aisha's voice cut in.

"Huh?" was his only response.

"You weren't here for awhile. Think of your dad."

"Now what makes you say that?"

"I know you better than you think, Detective. Did you notice the party stage-left?" She pointed to the last limo.

Craig couldn't believe what he saw: members of the Chinese mafia at Gercio's funeral.

"Hole-Lee shit! Now I've seen everything."

"I have to admit, Scalici, it was wise to come here today. Just do me a favor, and don't make your presence known 'til they start to leave."

"Give me some credit. I'm not that much of an asshole."

So they waited.

Craig kept his eye on Timmy Z, Marcella's husband. Maybe he wanted to get away from the family business. If Marcella was knocking off the competition and was now in cahoots with the Chinese mob, Timmy might want to get the hell out of there. But why come to his house? He had enough cash to fly the coop. Why would he want to make a deal with him directly? The kid. He wants to get the kid away from her too.

As the priest finished the blessing, Craig and Aisha got out of the car. Two dozen soldiers immediately turned their heads as the car doors slammed.

"So much for being discrete," Aisha remarked.

As they started to walk toward the crowd, Aisha began to see why

Craig was not nervous. With all these people looking on, Marcella wouldn't try a thing. In the past, they never had to worry about the mob hurting them. It would be bad for business. Lately though, they seemed more like warlords instead of businessmen. She turned and looked at the Chinese men, just in case.

Marcella looked directly at Craig, who stopped right before the close knit group by the casket. A hush fell over the crowd.

"What the hell are you doing here?" Marcella roared.

"Why I'm paying my respects, and you know how I respected your father," Craig answered in his best sarcasm.

"Get the fuck out of here!" she seethed, still holding Georgy's hand tight.

Aisha truly wanted to leave at that point. Clearly, this woman was not sane. At any moment that big red head of hers was going to yell out an order to shoot them, no matter who was watching.

"It's not your private property, Marcella. Actually I was hoping to see if his killer was here," he goaded her.

"You have no business being here," Timmy yelled out. "You're not even a homicide cop."

"Oh! The whipped one speaks!" Craig laughed. "You know Timmy, the little woman's done a bang up job here. Amazing how much she's *gained*, since poppa departed."

"What do you mean by that?" Marcella screamed. "You're saying I killed my own father?" She glared at Aisha. "You and this fat-ass nigger here."

"With the mass you're packing in that dress, hon, you shouldn't talk," Aisha fired back, knowing it would come back to haunt her.

From the corner of his eye, Craig saw Benny Esposito moving toward him. Before he could react, Tim was flying past Marcella and diving at Craig. He would have hit Craig square in the chest, but Craig simply shifted his stance and let Tim fly right past. Bringing his foot up at just the right moment, he sent Tim right to the ground.

"*Tim, no!*" Marcella screeched.

Craig reached down and yanked Tim up by his jacket. Benny and the rest kept their distance while Aisha pulled her weapon. As they all looked to her for a spilt second, Craig whispered to Tim, "Play along."

Everyone's attention went back to Craig and Tim.

"Assaulting an officer, huh? That's against the law, Timmy boy." Craig taunted.

"Screw you pig!" Tim spat in his face.

Craig threw him down on the ground and pulled out his cuffs.

"You bastard! Let go of him!" Marcella exploded.

Aisha was now terrified. Never had she pulled her gun. Now she was holding it on every gangster on the east coast and their crazy, evil queen. *Fuck you very much, Craig.*

Craig pulled Tim up hard and shoved him back toward the car, telling the crowd, "Carry on with your grieving, folks. Frank would have wanted it that way."

"You fucking asshole! I'll get you." Marcella snarled in a low voice.

"Am I going to wind up like your dad and Petey?" Craig smiled back at her.

"Don't talk to him! That's want he wants!" Tim shouted as Craig and Aisha took him back to the car.

"I'll get you out in an hour!" Marcella yelled to him, still clutching her son's small hand.

"Don't count on it!" Craig shouted back, roughly shoving Tim inside the car.

Aisha saw Marcella and became completely terrified. Was Marcella crazy enough to have them all shot? She looked like it, as God as her witness, that woman would be out to kill them all now. She hated to make the comparison, but she had the same look that Craig had when he thought Trish was taking Meredith away.

Craig was happy though; everything went according to plan, except for Trent Gold's camera secretly filming the whole thing.

•

The South Shore Mall had been beautifully air-conditioned for several years now. End of the summer sales abounded everywhere. Jeannine was in heaven. Detective Scalici had given her twenty bucks to buy new clothes for Meredith and twenty for herself. *Heaven!*

The mall was packed with frowning young kids being dragged by their mothers from sale to sale. Once in a while one poor mother would make the mistake of trying to buy Lee jeans instead of Levi's. On the teenage front, it was Smith's white painter's pains or the traditional Levi's again. These new Calvin Klein's jean were a joke. No self respecting Islip teen would *ever* wear designer jeans. At least according to Jeannine, and she knew clothes. *And...*she knew what was best for Meredith.

Whether people liked it or not, Jeannine was Meredith's real mother. She knew what was best for a little girl—shopping. Nevertheless, that last day at the beach still concerned her. Meredith was terrified of something or someone. Was it that Tim guy that showed up? Was it her grandparents or more of those gangsters? This very simple life of theirs had become very complex very quickly. And unless Meredith started to tell her more, she couldn't help her at all.

"Anything new, Meredith?" Jeannine asked, stopping in front of The Gap.

"Grandma and grandpa are moving to the beach year-round. They want to be with me more." Meredith was busy eyeing a denim jacket.

"Do they want you to move in with them?" she asked coyly, looking carefully at Meredith's expression.

"No, they said they'd never take me away from Daddy."

"That's good. How is your dad? He's been busy lately." Jeannine observed Meredith's demeanor stiffen.

"He's acting weird," she said.

"Oh?"

"He's acting different all the time. He's not the same."

"How so?"

"He hates talking to other people. He doesn't like it when Uncle Chip or Aunt Aisha calls."

"He doesn't like them?"

"No, he just doesn't like talking to them. I think it's his girlfriend," she said, looking up with eyes that would melt a drill sergeant.

"He has a girlfriend?" a startled Jeannine asked.

"Her name's Christina. He sees her every night."

"Meredith, your dad never leaves the house."

"Yes he does. He flies at night and meets her."

"Oh really, does he sprout wings?"

"He doesn't need them. I've seen him fly in my dreams sometime. He called her name out the other night from his bed. Christina."

With her hands full of bags, Jeannine moved Meredith to one of the benches. She plopped them down next to Meredith in hopes that no one tried to steal them, because Meredith now had her undivided attention.

"Meredith, the other day at the beach, you said that a woman wanted you. Does this Christina want to harm you?" Jeannine tried not to alarm the kid.

"I don't know. But there *is* a woman watching me. It gets really cold every time she does."

"Where is she when she's looking at you? Have I ever seen her?"

"You can't see her. She's in her cellar."

"Have you told your dad this?"

"No, he's been too busy. I didn't want to worry him."

With that, the beautiful air-conditioning in the mall kicked into over drive. All the shoppers immediately started to shiver, including Jeannine.

"She's back. She's watching us!" Meredith said, trembling.

"Let's get out of here. I don't like it in here either."

Leaving the bags on the ground, Jeannine picked up Meredith with ease and headed for the doors at the end of the mall. Complaints about the coldness started to be heard from the crowd. "What the hell is this crap!" and "It's fucking freezing in here!" were just some of the grumbling heard overpowering the Muzak.

"Jeannine, she's here. And she's really mad, too."

"There's no one here, kid. I just want to catch the bus before it leaves." Jeannine made a flat out sprint to the glass doors ahead. Desperately she ran, dodging old ladies and children that couldn't move out of her way fast enough. She could feel the coldness grabbing at her feet like a pack of wolves with icy fangs nipping at them. As she got to the door, she swung around to protect Meredith from the impact. Her back hit the door with full force, almost ripping it from its metal hinges.

They were free. Yet Jeannine did not feel the warmth of the sun on her face. Instead, it felt colder. The people outside all turned their heads. Down toward the end of Penney's, Jeannine saw the bus loading up with the last of its load.

"There are dogs behind us," Meredith said.

Jeannine turned around and saw a pack of gray-haired dogs standing about fifty feet away. Motionless, they glared at her.

Oh God, wolves.

Jeannine bolted for the bus. As she turned, she caught sight of them breaking into a run. All other sounds seemed to have disappeared as she heard the *click-click-click* of their paws hitting the pavement. The last passenger was getting on the bus just as she reached the back of it.

Click-click-click.

"Wait!" boomed from her lungs as she heard the air brakes hiss.

The bus pulled away for a split second, then screeched to a halt. She knew the wolves were just a foot or two behind her as she leaped into the doors.

"Close the doors!" she screamed.

The doors slammed behind her as the bus driver stared at them. "Are you okay?"

Jeannine looked back out and saw nothing. Even the people on the sidewalk seemed to have already gone back to their business as if nothing had happened.

"Um, yeah, I thought someone was chasing us," she panted, with Meredith in her arms.

"*She* was," Meredith whispered.

•

"She wasn't always like this," a solemn Tim explained to them. "She was into Stevie Nix and stuff like that."

The three of them sat on a bench in a synagogue. It was the only place Tim agreed to talk to them. Aisha didn't know what to make of the words coming out of the man's mouth. Normally she would drop the guy off at psych, but Craig was listening and believing every word. Reality as she knew it was begging to warp and change forever.

"She was beautiful too! I don't know when she began to cast spells, but one by one her dad's competitors began to disappear," he said, staring at the ground.

"Did she kill Petey and Terrell?" Craig asked, not sounding sympathetic at all.

Tim only nodded.

"What about her father?" Craig added coldly.

"I don't know. She runs hot and cold. She might have. Her powers are growing, and she did not like how he was running things. I could see her killing him, or me, then crying for doing so."

"But how did she do it?" Aisha asked, still trying to cling to reality.

"I told you, she's a witch!" He seemed offended. "*You* believe me." He looked right at Craig. "You've known for awhile."

"So what do you want us to do? We can't exactly use your testimony in court." Craig dodged his last statement.

"Help get me and my son to Israel. She can't harm me on holy ground. Once we're there, I'll give you evidence that you can use to put her away." He finally looked up.

"Evidence of what?" Aisha asked.

"Murder," he replied with a chill.

"Whose? A boss, a foot soldier, I thought everyone just disappeared," Craig spat out.

"My mother," came out of his mouth. "I saw her do it."

"Oh, dear God!" Aisha gasped.

"You *saw* it?" Craig asked, disgusted.

"She had been mysteriously sick for a long time. We had her at the mansion with us. I walked in as saw her smothering my mother with a pillow." Tim looked back down to the ground. "She was already dead."

"Why would she kill your mother?" Craig asked.

"Jealously. She is jealous of anyone that might take me or Georgy away from her."

"I hate to tell you this, but it will be your word against hers. That's not much, Timmy boy," Craig said. " We need more than that!"

"I taped her. I knew that both Georgy and I were in danger. So one night I hid a tape recorder in the nightstand. Before we went to sleep I asked her why she did it. She said it was because my mother was a bitch. Then she looked at me and told me never to mention it again, or she'd cut out my tongue."

"You have this on tape?" Both Craig and Aisha yelled at the same time.

"Yes. Will you help me?"

"Timmy, my boy, say hello to the wailing wall for me." Craig beamed.

"Now answer me this. Why do you hate me so much?" Tim asked with a new attitude. "I'm just trying to save my kid."

Craig stared right at him. Only Marcella's glare had ever shocked him like that.

"You want to know why? Because you knew what Marcella was all about. Maybe not the "Broom-Hilda" thing, but you *knew* they killed people. Was that okay with you? Just because they were good-looking and had money, that was okay with you? What about everybody they killed before your mother? What of the families of those people, Timmy boy? It's fine to kill people as long as its glamorous, right? It's all business, nothing personal. Newsflash, Timmy boy, if you kill someone, they take it personally."

"Craig!" Aisha yelled, seeing his anger grow.

Craig grabbed Tim by the hair and pulled his head up. He leaned in, right up to Tim's ear. "The only reason I have an atom of respect for you is because you're trying to save your kid. Otherwise I'd get the tape and let good ol' Benny know who ratted Marcella out."

Tim could only stare back.

"Now we'll help you. I promise. But you get me the tape now."

"I can't. She has informants throughout the force. If you don't bring me in soon, she'll know something's up."

"He's right," Aisha concurred.

"Trust me, her lawyers will have me out by five."

"Okay, but tomorrow, get me the tape, and I'll get you and the boy on a plane an hour later."

119

"But please be careful. What you said is true. I looked the other way. But she'll be after you two now, and the people you love."

"I gathered that. But tell me, can she turn into a dragon?" he asked.

"She might, I don't know."

•

The squad room was dead silent except for Chip who was at Craig's desk, being read the riot act over the phone.

"I don't know, ma'am. He should be back any minute now... Yes, I know who you are."

As Craig and Aisha entered the room with Tim, all eyes looked away. This was not a good sign.

"You always get a reception like this?" Tim asked under his breath.

"No, they usually growl at him," Aisha answered.

"Here he is now," Chip said loud enough for them to hear. Then he muzzled the phone. "Buddy, you have trouble! She's on a rampage."

"My mother-in-law?" he asked running over and taking the phone.

"No, your landlord." Chip passed off the phone.

At that point, Marcella could have danced in with a tutu on and no one would have noticed. Before Chip could tell him what else laid in wait, Craig got it with both barrels from Mrs. Snow.

"What the hell is going on? Are you screwing around in my house?" Julie Snow's voice shouted over the phone, loud enough for the whole squad room to hear.

"What?" was his only response.

"Your daughter was telling Jeannine that you're fucking some woman named Christina the last couple of nights. Well newsflash, she's now terrorizing both our daughters!"

"First of all, no one's been in the house except your family and mine. Now what do you mean Christina is terrorizing Meredith?" Craig asked on the verge of losing it.

"Today at the mall, this Christina woman..." Mrs. Snow stopped cold.

"Mrs. Snow, hello?" Craig said to the quiet phone. At that point, he looked up to see Rodham walking out of his office with a distraught Tanya and Jerry.

"Sorry for losing my temper, it happens once and awhile." Snow's voice suddenly entered his head again.

Now Craig remained silent. Tanya and Jerry looked over to him like two small children looking for their dad. From the door behind them stepped a man at least six-foot-five. By the size of the gut, the three-piece suite and crew cut, he knew it was a fed.

"Craig, are you still there?" Mrs. Snow's voice asked, remarkably comforting.

"Are the kids okay?" He asked as Rodham pointed right at him.

"Their fine, are you okay? Is everything alright?" she asked, sounding more like her mother.

"I'll let you know." He hung up.

Aisha, Chip and the rest of the squad room looked on as the man lumbered over to Craig.

"Detective Scalici?" the fed asked, stone-faced and a deep southern drawl.

Craig's automatic response to this type of situation kicked in. "Who the fuck wants to know?"

"Special Agent LeSorbe, Federal Bureau of Investigation," rolled off his tongue. "I hereby order you to hand over all material connected to your investigation of the Gercio crime family."

"Oh, fuck you, no." Craig replied.

"What's going on?" Tim asked Aisha.

"The shit finally hit the fan," she whispered.

"I don't need your permission detective," he repeated in that slow, laid back way that drove Craig nuts. "Out of courtesy I asked you first."

Craig's comeback was quick and in a mocking drawl. "Well, sir, you ain't getting them. So go back to Dixie and blow yourself."

Everyone cringed as Craig committed professional suicide before their eyes.

LeSorbe then turned to Rodham, unflinching. "I don't know how you folk's run things up here. But we handle things a little differently."

"Yes, its called being slow. That's one reason we won the war,"

Craig shot like a bullet and hit the mark.

All could see the Fed's face turn a slight red, as he continued with Rodham. "As per our discussion, please get me the files of officers Fernandez and Mahoney."

Tanya and Jerry looked to each other then back to Craig.

"Hold on here. What do you want with them?" Craig asked, realizing where this was all going.

The Fed looked back at him with a cockfighting winner's grin. "I must commend you, Detective, you're slipperier than oiled pig shit. You've been making a mockery of the law for years now, and somehow got away with it. Magically, you managed to side step the shit holes this whole time. Your young friends here though, have all sorts of blemishes, to the scale that your district attorney should get involved."

Jerry exploded, "That's bullshit—!"

Craig shut him up with one look. Behind them, he saw Devaney holding a stack of files and giving him the finger. They got him.

"Okay, you're welcome to it. You already know where the papers are, I'll bring the rest in from home." Craig looked the man in his face.

Turning to Aisha, the Fed cocked his brow. "And you must be Barlow."

"And what gave me away?" Aisha sparred coldly, knowing the look of bigotry immediately.

"You remind him of the plantation," Craig jabbed in.

Both Aisha and LeSorbe gave him a look to kill.

"Enough!" Rodham yelled, then walked to Craig and spoke in a low tone. "Go home and cool down. He wants me to take your badge, too."

"Now if you don't mind," LeSorbe added, "I'll take their prisoner into federal custody."

"No!" Tim yelled. "That's not the deal!"

"You have no choice, son." LeSorbe grabbed his arm.

"Don't worry, Tim, you'll be fine. He doesn't know what he's getting into," Craig reassured him. "A promise is a promise."

"Sir, will you kindly have your men escort my prisoner to my car?" LeSorbe asked Rodham.

"I'm sorry, but they're all very busy," Rodham replied.

LeSorbe looked around the room. "They don't look busy to me."

With that, every officer in the room stood up and filed out the door. One by one they patted Craig and Aisha on the back. Chip even went as far as whistling The Battle Hymn of the Republic. Finally, Devaney walked over and grabbed Tim by the arm. "I'll take him." Devaney walked out and Aisha followed.

"Go home, Craig. I'll see you tomorrow," Rodham instructed, then gave LeSorbe a look and retreated to his office, leaving the two alone.

"Like I said, boy, I don't know what kind of spell you had over these people, but I just broke it," LeSorbe gloated with pure hatred in his voice.

"Word's of advice you racist dick," Craig smiled. "Watch out for what you don't know."

"And what's that supposed to mean?" he asked, waiting for Craig to mouth off again.

"Hold on to Timmy too long, and you'll see," Craig whispered confidently.

•

"What the hell are you going to do now?" Aisha asked, tearing up and still furious at him. "How are you going to get him away from the feds *and* get the tape?"

"Marcella will get him out in an hour or so. I hope no one gets hurt in the process, even Foghorn Leghorn back there," Craig said, pulling onto the expressway.

The chill that came over her was immediately noticed, and it wasn't due to a spell.

"I know this whole witchcraft mumbo-jumbo is odd. But if you can come up with another explanation, I'm all ears."

"I don't care about the delusions the two of you are having!" she shot back. "You just know it all, don't you?"

"Alright, I'm an asshole! I admit it," he said, merging into traffic.

"You're more than that! You just had to butt heads with that guy! If you just took it like a normal person, maybe we could have worked something out!"

"Come on. That ass-wipe would not have given an inch!"

"Well we won't know now! There are other ways of doing something than your way! You *do not* know it all!"

Out of the entire population of the planet, only Aisha Barlow could erupt and put Craig in his place.

"I never said I knew it all, but I'm damn close. Why are you defending that racist asshole anyway?"

"Because I have to work with racist assholes everyday! If I didn't, I'd be out of work! You forget where I'm from, where it was that the school board's job was to keep us Negroes away from town and all the white kids."

"Come on. There's only a few Devaney's in the group. People may talk inappropriately, but they're not all racists."

"Yes, you are right. And most racists may never use racist language. They're not all like LeSorbe. Now just shut up about this. You just don't know," she warned.

"This isn't the hicks up here. It's…"

Before he could finish, she hauled off and smacked him up side the head.

"Ow!" he cried, almost as much from surprise as pain.

"Just shut up! You don't know anything about this!" she warned him again.

"I do understand. My family emigrated from—"

"*Stop right there!* You never had to explain to your son why he was called a nigger! That's not part of your world, and never will be!"

"I've been called nigger-lover!" He smiled at her.

At that point Aisha wanted to plant her fist in the side of the asshole's face. If he hadn't been driving, she might have.

"Time to open your eyes, Craig. Pull off at the next exit," she insisted.

"If you want. What's there?" he asked, throwing on his turn signal.

"What I have to deal with."

•

124

Millionaire's Mile was a stretch of the Jericho Turnpike famous for its upscale stores. It wasn't Rodeo Drive, but close. Aisha had Craig pull the Mustang up along a span of shops, all of which had a round canvas awning. She then gave him very specific instructions.

"Now you see that shop right there?" She pointed across the street.

Craig looked over and saw a typical looking jewelry store.

"Yes, ma'am."

"Now I'm going to go in there. *You* stay here for seven minutes. Then come in and just walk up to the counter. *Do not* ask for any help," she instructed. "Understand?"

"I un-der-stand."

"Now, how do I look?" she asked.

"Pissed."

"My outfit, you moron!"

Craig looked at her suit. She wore a nice blazer with a knee length skirt, and a pretty scarf was wrapped around her neck. To him it looked perfectly fine. "Looks snazzy."

"It better look snazzy! It cost me more than what you pay for five of what you call suits! Now remember, seven minutes. Do not ask for help," she instructed again and left.

Craig watched her as she walked across the street. She was right, she looked better than 'snazzy', she did look good, polished even. Christina had that same look.

Watch it Craiger! His head told him.

She pulled on the glass doors of the posh jewelry store.

•

Seven minutes passed of Craig of wondering what fucking happened with Meredith and Jeannine, and how Christina's name got mentioned. The whole witchcraft thing with Gercio confirmed his ideas and proved that he wasn't going crazy. Any other day he would be elated that he wasn't bonkers. As long as he could get his hands on Timmy's tape, he could put everything right. Nothing like seeing Marcella get what's coming to her. If his hunch was right, if she was exposed as a witch, she'd be powerless. Then the shits like Devaney and LeSorbe would get both barrels. And his in-laws would...

Before he knew it, ten minutes had passed.

Shit.

The inside of the jewelry store was like the outside, flawless. The glass counters were all perfectly parallel. The carpet was a soft cream that felt comfortable even with shoes on. Aisha was standing by a counter where dim fluorescent lights showed off thousand of dollars worth of diamond necklaces. A thin tall man with a pointed chin stood and watched her from the other end. His suit smacked of lots o' money, one that would undoubtedly impress his in-laws. Immediately he walked over to Craig.

"May I help you, sir?" the man asked from his ferret-like face.

Craig looked over to Aisha, who was looking back at them both. He got the point.

"I believe the lady was here first," Craig answered.

"Oh, she's just looking," he said.

With that, Aisha turned and walked out. At first Craig wanted to make an obnoxious comment about the man's behavior, but just walked out instead.

•

"You're right, I'm sorry," Craig finally said to break the silence. They had already been back on the expressway for a good ten minutes.

"Now do you see? You never would have known what my children and I will go through for the rest of our lives. It's another world that you will never understand," Aisha said. "Don't get me wrong. You're a good man. But don't think you understand everything. Things exist right under your nose and you don't realize it."

"I'm sorry."

"Now this whole witchcraft thing. Could it be possible that Marcella could belong to some cult? Maybe more extensive than her mob ties?" she asked, trying to reason with him.

"This isn't something I just came up with. Weird things have been going on. Just one too many for a logical explanation." He confessed, "Okay, I've been having these freaked out dreams lately. Just as I think I'm going to remember them completely, I forget them again."

Aisha froze. The nightmares she'd been having herself were very clear in her mind. "What do you remember?"

"Flying, and Christina."

"Who is this Christina?" she asked.

"She's a professor at C. W. Post. She's an expert on different folklore." He felt that Christina could better explain it all to her.

"I've been having nightmares too. And I remember every last moment of them. Does this Christina know anything about psychology?"

"Beats me, I've only met her once."

"Once? The way you talked, it seemed you knew her for a while."

Craig clicked on the turn signal and started to pull off the expressway again.

"What are you doing?" she asked, bewildered.

"This is the exit for the campus, why don't we just go ask her what she knows?"

Aisha saw his face soften at that moment, almost light up. He had a crush on this woman. Like an adolescent, pimple-faced boy in love with the homecoming queen.

"Funny how the exit is right here." Her own curiosity was now aroused. There was some *mojo* at work here. Now that she saw it for herself, she began to look at other possible worlds she never noticed. Perhaps witches and dragons were real.

"Don't forget. You brought her up just now," he pointed out.

"I sure did, didn't I?"

Chapter 9

SPECIAL EDITION

"What do you mean he's free to go?" LeSorbe hollered over the phone. "How the hell did they even know he was in federal custody?"

"They knew somehow and got him sprung," the regional director informed him.

"What type of pussy fags are you up here?" he ranted. "I'm not going to let that Jew boy out of my sight!"

"Who do you think you're talking to, mister? I don't care who your uncle is, you obey orders just like the rest of us!" The director replied, actually being afraid of Judge LeSorbe and what good ol' boy strings he could pull.

"I'm talkin' to a no-balls momma's boy who couldn't piss his way out of a paper bag!" LeSorbe spat, meaning every word.

"If Zimmer is not released immediately, I will have you up for insubordination!" the director ordered.

"You think I'm worried 'bout a write up. Wipe your ass with it for all I care. If they want 'um, they'll have to take 'um!" he yelled.

With that, LeSorbe slammed the phone down hard enough to make it ring. He looked down to Tim. In the small cube of an office, he had placed him in a chair, handcuffed with very little room to move. The desk and LeSorbe's bulk made it extremely claustrophobic. LeSorbe was the man. Nothing was going to get past him, and if this scrawny little shit could deliver a couple of mob bosses, he was going to get them.

"So tell me about this deal you had with the Italian stallion back there," LeSorbe asked, towering over Tim.

"Th-there was no deal," Tim answered meekly.

LeSorbe belted him right in the gut. The pain was sharp at first, then excruciating, like a Mac truck just slammed into him. All air was instantly gone from his lungs.

"That's not what you said back there, boy. Now I want to know what you were going to give them." LeSorbe grabbed the cuffs locked behind Tim's back. "Or you're going to be one of those convicts that have to be subdued," he said, and then pulled up on the cuff. With the wind still knocked out of him, Tim couldn't even yell.

The phone rang.

"What the fuck?" LeSorbe picked up the phone with his usual finesse. "Who the hell is it?"

Marcella's voice answered softly, "Me."

LeSorbe heard her voice on the phone and in the room at the same time. He looked up to see Marcella, still in her black funeral dress, standing in the doorway.

"Jesus Christ! You can't be up here!" he shouted at her.

Big mistake.

"But I am. Now you were told to let him go. You should always obey your superiors."

"They have no balls!" he hollered with a red face near explosion.

"Neither do you," she grinned, removing one of her black silk gloves. She was suddenly in front of him, her hand firmly gripping his scrotum.

LeSorbe could only gasp as he felt her nails growing longer and imbedding around his testicles.

"See what happens to those who cross me?" she cackled, then ripped them off his body.

LeSorbe's dropped to his knees wailing in agony. Marcella held them up before his eyes. "That's what you get for being an asshole."

Magically, the handcuffs fell off Tim's wrists as he watched LeSorbe curled up on the floor. Blood was gushing from behind his fingers as they gasped the mutilated area. Tim stood and Marcella dropped LeSorbe's manhood on the ground.

"You okay, dear?" she asked tenderly.

"Um, yeah," he answered, watching LeSorbe continue to cry in pain.

"The way you stood up for me at the cemetery was beautiful. I thought you didn't love me anymore," she said with a tear in her eye, putting the glove back on her bloody hand.

"Of course I love you. But what about this?" he asked, looking at LeSorbe, not daring to show his own fear of the woman.

"They'll never see him. At least not until they tear down the building." she said, then walked out the door.

LeSorbe watched as the two left. Marcella closed the door behind her, and then it disappeared. Pain turned to panic as he stared at nothing but bare walls where the door was. With no windows, no one could see in or out. Desperately, he grabbed the phone with his bloody hands and pressed zero.

"Help me!" he screamed into the receiver.

Marcella's voice answered, "Sorry, your number cannot go through. No need to try again."

LeSorbe began to cry, knowing he would never be found.

•

She's beautiful, Aisha thought. No wonder Craig had a thing for her after just one meeting. She could tell she had a thing for Craig too. These were two people meant to be together. They were meant to have children and be in love. Like two parts of a jigsaw puzzle that were finally united.

"Detectives, I have to admit that you really bring some glamour to my job," Christina joked.

"I wish I brought some to ours," Craig replied.

Despite all the chaos, Aisha knew that Christina was Craig's destiny, and he deserved it. Her life was no bed of roses, yet she always compared her life to his and felt much better.

"I'm so glad we finally get to meet," Aisha smiled

"Finally? We met only once and I made a mess of things." Christina answered a little concerned.

"Aisha is not only my partner, she also my yenta mother," Craig threw in.

"You need one, if yenta means black and concerned," Aisha scolded.

"Basically, it does," Christina laughed.

"So tell me more about witches." Aisha tried to make the conversation transition as smooth as possible. "You had said that their magic is close to that of dragons."

"That's right. According to some legends. One legend states that gargoyles are the offspring of dragons and witches." She paused, not liking how the two detectives were looking at her. "What is going on? You told me before you felt people were pretending to be dragons. What? Are they pretending to be witches now?"

"Professor Lee, I'm as grounded to mother Earth as a tulip bulb," Aisha confessed. "But what I've seen and experienced lately defies reality. I'm not saying that Craig is right about these dragons and witches. Yet I'm beginning to open my mind."

"Is there one witch in particular you're talking about?" Christina shifted her body, clearly suspicious and skeptical.

"Yes, Frank Gercio's daughter, Marcella," Craig answered.

Aisha noticed the relief that reentered Christina.

"Well," Christina offered, "one thing I can tell you is that according to all the folklore I've read, if a witch uses her magic for evil, it will come back to her even more so."

"Can they turn into dragons?" Craig asked.

"I don't know. It would have to be a very powerful witch." Christina appeared nervous again.

"Are you a witch, Professor?" Aisha asked point blank.

Both Christina and Craig stopped dead.

"I beg your pardon?" Christina sounded like a child caught fibbing.

"You seem very nervous when we talk about witchcraft. So, are you a witch?" Aisha asked again.

"Aisha?" Craig's eyes flew to Aisha's, appalled..

She knew he'd explode soon if Christina didn't fess up soon.

"No!" Christina answered, looking away from Aisha's eyes. "But...I do *see* things."

"What?" Craig's attention flew back to Christina.

"It's not something I talk about. Throughout my whole life, I could see things in my dreams, or know when bad things were going to happen." She looked at Craig, "And good things."

"Professor, I've been having some real bad dreams lately, real doosies involving my kids and family," Aisha said, then looked to Craig. "Even this knucklehead. In everyone of them, they're dead."

Craig sat back as the drama unfolded between the two women.

"It's not from me," Christina assured her. "But if the folklore is true, you might be under the spell of the witch."

"Then how come she's killed other people and not us?" Detective Barlow asked.

"If your souls are good, it will not be easy for her," Christina said softly. "Or if you pray, or if someone is blocking her spells."

"Could that someone be you, Professor?" Aisha asked.

Christina did not answer. Instead she walked over to the window and looked out over the campus.

"I'm not a witch, Detective. If you have anymore specific questions about folklore, by all means call me. I do have a class in a few minutes, so I'm afraid I must ask you to leave."

"Thank you, Professor. It was very nice to meet you." Aisha smiled. "I think you're a lovely person."

"Yes, thank you," Craig added, at a loss for words.

"I hope everything turns out well for you both." Christina replied, not facing them as they left. She watched them leave from her window and hated herself for lying.

•

"What just happened back there?" Craig asked Aisha as they got back into the Mustang.

"Detective work," she replied. "Even though reality as I knew it took a flying leap, I can still tell when someone is hiding something. She should have told you this before now."

"It's only the second time we've met!" he objected, closing the door.

"Bullshit! Somehow she's been seeing you before this. Maybe she's been coming to you in your dreams. She's in love with you, and if you don't get your head blown off, you'll realize you have it bad for her.

"Wait a minute, an hour ago you had me ready for the booby hatch. Now you're saying I'm dating someone in my dreams. And what do you mean, get my head blown off?" he asked, trying to make sense of his partner's new attitude.

"I opened your eyes and you opened mine, now give me your hand," she said

"Oh no. There's no call for this!"

"Give me your hand," she insisted, taking her Bible out of her purse.

"You know I don't believe in this stuff!" he protested again.

"You got me to believe in witches and dragons. You can believe in the good book. Now you place your hand on this bible or I'll do it *for* you!"

He hated it when she made him do this, and he always succumbed. So he placed his hand on her bible and waited for the demand.

"Now swear to me on the Lord's word that you will not go to get that tape from Zimmer."

"But—"

"No buts, swear to me!" she ordered.

"I swear not to try and get the tape."

"Good, now you be careful. Once Marcella gets her hubby back, she'll be gunning for all of us. Even your new girlfriend back there."

"She's not my girlfriend," he insisted.

"No, she's your soul mate. I have a little *mojo* too. I know these things."

"Yes, ma'am." He knew that he didn't swear about getting Tim and the boy out of the country like he promised.

●

It was odd seeing the green Chevy in the driveway. Julie Snow was waiting for Craig on the porch. She had apparently evicted her mother to get the seat. For her to take time off from work, something had to be important. He tried calling her several times, but there was no answer. Now he was going to get them whether he wanted to or not.

"I thought you'd be home early," she said. "I'm sorry for calling you like that. I hope everything is okay?"

"It's pretty shitty, to be frank. What I want to know is what happened to our daughters?" he asked her, stepping up on the porch.

"Jeannine called me at work terrified. She claims that there's a witch trying to kill Meredith."

Thoughts of Marcella ran through his mind. The main thing was not to let other people know. Mrs. Snow would probably track Marcella down and try to kill her.

"I could understand Meredith thinking there a witch in her closet, but what makes Jeannine believe it?" Craig asked, hoping Marcella wasn't after Meredith and Jeannine.

Please God, let it all be in their heads.

"They were in the mall and a pack of wolves chased them onto a bus!" she said coldly.

That's not in their heads.

"Mrs. Snow, I'm sorry. There might be people evil enough to harm our kids. If you want, I'll leave tonight and stay with friends. I'll move out as soon as I can." He added, "As far as witchcraft is concerned, I feel people may go through great lengths to give the illusion of something magical."

"You don't have to move detective. Jeannine is staying with friends, and my mother is with some of my aunts." She smiled, "Playing lookout for you gave her a good thrill."

"Now about Christina Lee. She's never even been here, I barely know

134

the woman. She's consulting on a case I'm working on," he explained, not knowing if he was lying or not.

"Apparently you've been calling her name out at night. If she does come over, Detective, I disapprove of her spending the night," she admonished him.

Craig never had a bad thing to say to his landlord. Now he felt like telling her to mind her own fucking business. He paid a hefty amount in rent; he could do whatever he damn well pleased.

"You'll never see her past ten," is what finally came out of his mouth.

•

"Meredith, is there anything you'd like to tell me?" Craig asked his daughter as he took the Jiffy-Pop off the stove. Craig felt she had some pangs of guilt for her actions. There was a special on TV that Meredith really wanted to see. Nothing seemed more appealing to him than a quiet night of popcorn, TV, and his daughter.

"Didn't Mrs. Snow tell you?" she answered, getting the butter out of the fridge.

It was time to play it cool. He took out the big blue Pyrex bowl that had been the official Scalici popcorn bowl since Meredith was born. Briefly, Craig had a fond memory of Trish. She used to balance the bowl on her pregnant belly and call herself a coffee table. If Marcella did kill Trish, he'd make sure she'd get tried for two murders.

"She did, but I want you to tell me what happened. I don't think Jeannine has the detective mind you have," he said, pouring the popcorn in the bowl.

"I think there's a witch trying to get me," she said, cutting a big slab of butter.

"Don't you think I should know about this?" he asked, trying hard not to be cross.

"Get real, Daddy. If I told you a witch was after me, you'd think I'm mental. Besides, it doesn't matter, she can't get me anyway."

"Oh, why's that?" he asked, throwing the butter in the corn.

"She just can't. As a matter of fact, it's getting harder for her to find me. I think she looks for Jeannine instead. She knows I'm always with her," she said matter-of-factly, as if it were nothing. "Hurry, Daddy, I think you'd like this show."

"And what is this show called?" he asked, moving to the living room, where he had the book conveniently placed.

"Trent Gold's Special Edition. You know, your friend from TV."

"He's not my friend, dear." He turned on the tube. "Have you seen Daddy's new book? It's about dragons."

"No." Looking at it triggered her interest. "Can I read it?"

"Sure. I know the author you know."

She looked at the name, and then flipped to the back. "She's pretty. Is this your friend Christina?"

"Yes. Have you ever seen her before? Even in your dreams?"

"Um, no. I don't see anybody when I'm dreaming. I'm flying too high." She smiled, popping a kernel in her small mouth.

Craig's anticipation grew tenfold, was Meredith having the same dream? "Flying? How are you flying? On a winged horse or a dragon?"

"No, by myself."

Just then, Trent Gold appeared on the screen in front of them like a very unwelcome guest. Instead of his usual tailored look, he wore a pink polo shirt and tan Chinos. Craig figured it was to try and give him the "I'm just like you" look.

"Good Evening, welcome to Trent Gold's Special Edition." He grinned with more teeth than one of Christina's dragons. "You're probably used to seeing me cracking tough news stories and exposing corruption." The camera angle changed and so did his stance. "Tonight is different though. Tonight we'll look into the paranormal. Are there forces out there beyond our control? Are government officials covering up the truth?" The screen cut to the alleyway where Petey died.

Craig gasped a kernel into his windpipe as he saw himself on TV.

"Look, Daddy, it's you." Meredith was elated.

"Oh shit!" he wheezed.

"Daddy!" Meredith protested, knowing she'd get sent to her room if she had said that.

"A blimp, a big magical blimp with monkey pilots," Craig's voice spoke from the tube.

"This is Detective Craig Scalici from the NYPD. Notice the sky above the alley, though. This was not seen when it was broadcast live. But on tape, look at what appears," Gold's voice narrated.

Craig watched in disbelief as the image of the eye appeared in the sky above him.

"Cool, Daddy! Did you see it that night?" Meredith asked her father, who was in the early stages of shock.

"This is no trick folks, this was recorded on our own camera. And this isn't all. Watch as we encounter more of these odd occurrences as we follow Detective Scalici." Craig's image appeared on the screen again. "So stay with us folks as we take you on a ride into the bizarre."

"Jesus H. Christ!" Mrs. Snow's voice echoed from upstairs.

"Look, Daddy, you're famous now," Meredith beamed.

•

"That fucking asshole!" Marcella cried out. "How the hell did they get that?"

Like Craig, Marcella too, wanted a night alone with the family. Now that she had Tim back, and her father was now laid to rest, she could get on with things. The way Tim had stood up for her at the cemetery had not only dispelled any doubt she had of him, it had increased her love for him twenty-fold. The three of them were going to have a night where there was no worry of the outside world, where everything was put on hold for them to unite as the family she always wanted to have.

She knew what her people thought of her and her looks. With all the power she had amassed, she still couldn't lose a single fucking pound. That bothered her a bit, yet everything else was coming up roses. No one was a threat to her anymore. The Dragon was her biggest worry. His mind was the strongest, though, she thought. This whole business with her dad was unnerving. Then again, she knew using her powers had their drawbacks. In the meantime, her family was in order and nestled in for the night. Bad enough she had to see Scalici, then when her one spell literally looked back at her, she felt invaded. In a sense she was raped. Scalici had forced himself on her once too often.

"Bennaaaaaaah!" she screamed.

Within moments, Benny was in the family room. His gun was drawn at first, since no one was ever allowed in the family room except family. For her to call him, there had to be trouble, big trouble.

"What is it, ma'am?" Benny asked, looking around for an intruder.

"Get me The Dragon now! I need him to go to work for me!"

"Yes boss. What happened?" he asked, holstering his gun.

"He's gone too far this time," she smoldered, seeing film of Craig at the cemetery.

On the couch, Tim held Georgy in his arms praying Craig would make good on his promise.

•

"Oh my God," Barbara spoke slowly to Chip. "Is that real?"

"Of coarse it's not real," Chip replied. "I was there. There was no floating eye!"

Their three little ones, of course, turned up from their positions on the carpet, where they had watched TV with chins embedded in their hands.

"Is that what Uncle Craig called a monkey blimp?" their oldest girl, Sammy, asked.

"No, there was no eye, there was no blimp! Uncle Craig was just being a wise-ass, honey," he tried to explain.

"No, just a frozen body in the middle of summer," Barbara added, crossing her arms.

"A frozen body? Cool!" Ian, the youngest, grinned.

"No, not cool. And he wasn't frozen!" Chip reiterated, giving Barbara a chastising look.

"Kids, go in the kitchen and get some ice cream. As much as you want," Barbara offered.

As if they were beamed directly to the kitchen, their three darlings were gone in a heartbeat.

"What's going on with Craig? And you for that matter?" Barbara inquired in the tell-me-now mode.

"Like the show said, hon, the bizarre. I'm worried about him. Ever since Gercio was offed like that, stranger and stranger shit's been happening to him. I think Trish's dying is affecting him more than he admits. There's this woman he's been seeing, I think, that's been playing with his mind."

"Are *you* okay?" she asked, as the anxiety in her grew.

"Honestly," he confessed. "I haven't gotten a good night's sleep since the night Gercio got it."

"That next night was the night Craig slept over," she figured out loud, and then saw her rock of a husband begin to tremble. She put her arm around him and felt every goose bump rise on his cold clammy skin. "Well tomorrow, you're calling in. And don't worry about Craig, he'll deal with this his own way." She hoped she was right.

•

Aisha already had the Rosary beads clutched in her hands when she saw herself and Craig arresting Zimmer at the cemetery. When Trent Gold was shown at the airstrip where Trish had jumped, she started praying to Saint Jude, the saint of lost causes.

•

Sandra and Thornton watched as Trent Gold interviewed the bum that was their daughter's last boyfriend. They froze when they saw the house where their granddaughter and son-in-law lived on public TV. Thor was immediately on the phone to his cronies at the network.

•

Alone, Trent watched with delight as he destroyed Craig's life on TV. From his office, which he expected to be expanded soon, he laughed thinking about the sky-high ratings he was going to get. From the win-

139

dows he looked out upon the entire city that was watching his show. It worked out beautifully that there was no game that night. The new fall shows were still a week away. That meant that he was the only game in town. He knew that his days as a serious news reporter were over, but who cared? The network was sure to get flack on this, but with the new wonderful world of syndication, he was going to be coast to coast. If he ran out of good super natural mumbo-jumbo, hell, he'd just make it up. On top of it all, he had the last laugh on that dickhead detective.

Something outside caught his eye.

Trent looked out, but didn't see anything at first. Then he noticed that a whole city block had gone dark. Right after that, another, then another. All the blocks between his building and the East River started going out one by one in a path directly toward him. Before he knew it, his room was dark as night.

"Damn it!" he screamed, thinking the broadcast would be quashed, and threw his remote somewhere into the darkness. Something of glass shattered out of sight. Just as his anger started to radiate into madness, he remembered that they didn't broadcast from his building anymore.

Now chuckling, he felt his way over to the desk in hopes of finding the phone. He didn't even have the benefit of moonlight to help him look. Patting his hands around, he felt the smooth plastic of the phone. He was happy to hear the soft ring as he hit it, confirming his find.

Outside the sound of the city started to die out as the wind began to pick up. There must be one hell of a storm blowing through. He looked back to the window to see the two orange eyes staring back at him. At first that was all he saw. They were tremendous. The black pupils themselves took up the whole floor-length window. The irises radiated outward in wavelike streaks of red and yellow on an orange background. Now his eyes adjusted to see the pattern of scales in swirls as they ran forward into a snout pressed against the glass. The condensation vapor from the nostrils appeared and disappeared off the window as the head of the dragon hovered before him.

Whoosh.

In an instant, the head was gone and the white wall of the creature's belly was flying upward. The windows themselves pressed outward a bit as if a tremendous vacuum was trying to suck them away.

Trent's whole body had been fossilized into stone. He couldn't gasp if he had wanted to. All he could do is watch as the dragon's tail whizzed by out of sight. In less then a second, he saw the dragon up in the sky, doing a back flip. It twirled around twice, and then started charging, swooping, diving—right at him. His frozen feet finally broke free from their paralysis and he bolted to the door. Luckily it was right where he had remembered it was. Fear crushed his chest as he swung the door open and ran into the hall illuminated in emergency floodlights.

He was alone.

The rest of the staff left early for the weekend. At the far end of the hall, the exit sign glowed eerily, almost the same color as the eyes of the "Thing" he just saw. Running to the stairs, the entire building shook as if a wrecking ball had hit it.

Trent fell to the ground as the wall and floor behind him crumbled away and the night sky was suddenly behind him. Inches away from his feet was now a sixty-story drop to the city below. Amazingly the exit sign still beckoned in front of him. Desperately, he tried to crawl to it as two massive claws pounced down on either side of him, digging deep into the concrete. The light from the sign actually reflected in the smooth black talons. On his stomach, Trent lay motionless. The wind from the night air blew through the hair he was primping just an hour ago. In the background he could hear the city traffic below, in between each breath the beast took.

He had just enough room to turn himself over. It was as if the creature had wanted him to. For a moment, he looked at those hideous eyes again. They almost seemed to be human, like a woman's. They disappeared as its great jaw opened, revealing the long rows of bleached white teeth. The hot stench of its breath enveloped him like sickening fog of rotting meat.

Before he knew it, he was being crushed by walls of warm slime. His shoulder cried out in a lightening bolt of pain. Oddly, he knew with a feeling of absolute certainty that it had just been bitten off as the dragon swallowed him.

He didn't care; he just wanted to die before he reached the stomach.

Chapter 10

THE DRAGON VISITS

As if cued by the end of the show, Craig's phone rang. He thought about taking it off the hook on the last commercial break, yet he just couldn't move at the time.

"Craig?" Rodham's voice asked on the phone in a way Craig never heard it, scared. "What is this on the TV?"

"I don't know, sir. At least fifty men were there, no one saw an eye floating in the air."

On the TV, Craig saw a teletype scroll along the bottom. "From Live Action Weather Team: There is a severe thunderstorm and tornado watch for the entire metro area until 11:00 PM."

Rodham added, "Well, the news just keeps getting better, pal—LeSorbe has disappeared."

"What? Where's Zimmer?" Craig immediately asked.

"Back at Alder with Marcella. Apparently he wouldn't give Zimmer up even though the lawyers sprung him. Now he's vanished, like Gercio and your wife." As he spoke his voice cracked like an adolescent caught shoplifting.

"What are you insinuating, sir?" Craig asked, his temper just beginning to show splotches of red.

"It doesn't take a fucking rocket scientist to find the common denominator here, Craig. I know you well enough to know you would never harm someone without being provoked, but..."

"But what?"

"You have a temper and somehow these people who piss you off are being killed! You or one of our own might be next! Do yourself a favor and take Meredith away." He paused to take a breath and continued as if he was forcing the words out. "I had nightmares last night. People I care for dying. Get away from here, now."

Craig knew Rodham was right. He was concerned for him and the rest of the police pack. He looked to Meredith sitting cross-legged on the floor, picking at the remaining corn kernels.

"And, Craig," he added, "if it means anything, everybody respects what you did for Tanya and Jerry. You're not the stuck-up asshole anymore."

"No, I'm the 'getting fucked up the butt' asshole."

He didn't care if Meredith heard. Rodham hung up with out even saying goodbye. Craig almost put the phone back on the hook from habit, but then laid it on the table. He wanted to go and tell Mrs. Snow they were leaving and that she should do the same. He was surprised whackos hadn't come to gawk at the house, like a new Amityville Horror. He looked to Meredith and saw a figure in the doorway. Before he could reach for his gun, which he now carried all the time, he saw Christina standing at his opened front door. Meredith had let her in.

"Meredith Ann! What did I say about letting strangers in?" Craig scolded, watching Christina's eyes blink from the force of his voice.

"But it's the lady from your dragon book!" Meredith protested without being startled.

"I'm sorry Craig, I, I, only knocked," Christina tried to explain.

Craig's heart instantly warmed seeing the two together. Everything became clear again.

"No, I'm sorry. Everything in my life right now was just broadcast to the entire New York area."

"I saw. That's why I came to your home. We must talk." She was trembling ever so slightly. It turned him on like a shock from a bare wire.

"I was just about to leave..."

"Leave?" Meredith protested. "I thought we were going to watch TV tonight?"

"We are, honey. I just don't want to spend the night here. People might bother us," he said calmly. "I just want to tell my landlady."

"Where are you going to go? I don't think a motel is the best idea?" Christina warned. "You just need one person to see you and tell the news people."

Craig laughed, "It's not *that* bad."

"It will be. Other events have taken place. My house is just ten minutes away from here. You are more than welcome to come." She looked down to Meredith. "Both of you."

Craig didn't bother to debate the fact. He needed to get away from the public fuckin' floating eye that was now on him.

"Come on, Daddy, we can have that slumber party you promised me. Your girlfriend can tell us dragon stories."

"She's *not* my girlfriend!" Craig insisted. "Now go get your bag, like you were going to Grandma's."

Meredith skipped out of the room, leaving the two alone.

Craig finally spoke, breaking the awkward silence. "Considering we just met, our paths keep coming together."

"Did we just meet?" Christina asked. Her beautiful dark eyes peered straight into his soul. "I haven't been a hundred percent honest with you." Like being stuck by a needle, Christina looked to the window.

Craig knew trouble was on the other side.

"They're here," Christina whispered.

Before another thought could pop in his head, Craig dove and tackled Christina into the foyer. Bullets flew through the window and pelted the walls of the living room. He could feel the lead brushing the hairs on the back of his head as he landed on top of Christina. Despite what was going on, the feel of her delicate body beneath him aroused him even more.

Meredith!

"Meredith! Stay on the floor!" he yelled, pulling his gun out. His pounding heart froze when she didn't answer at first.

"Daddy, what was that?" Meredith's voice asked out loud after an eternity. "Fireworks?"

"*Get under the bed! now!*" Christina's voice blasted from under Craig.

The amount of power from the frail body was surprising. His ears would be ringing for a while. Face to face, she looked into him.

"There are three of them. One's in the back waiting for us," she said calmly.

He didn't bother to ask her how she knew that. First thing was to get rid of the one in the back, before he broke into the kitchen. He crawled off Christina and hit the light switch. The living room went dark except for the TV.

"Stay on the ground," he told Christina, wriggling his way to the kitchen like a snake. Christina stayed put as both the TV and foyer light went dark.

At first, Craig thought whoever was outside had cut the power, then the peal of thunder rolled overhead. As he made it to the kitchen, he could see that the neighbor's lights were out. This wasn't good. They might confuse the gunshots with thunder or fireworks. It was Labor Day weekend. The linoleum felt cool under his hands as he entered his kitchen. Even the white cabinets and floor could be seen in the darkness. The silence was absolute. There was no sound or light whatsoever.

Craig held his gun to the back door. He wanted to give himself space to react. Part of his mind tried to see where they would be outside, probably in the shrubs or behind Mrs. Snow's massive Chevy. In the blackness, he could feel his pupils dilating so he could take in as much light as he could. With his next heartbeat, a flash of lightening filled the room. Silent white light engulfed the room. To the side, he saw the figure of a head at the far window. With reflex, he fired. The bullet left his gun just as the clap of thunder hit the house. The house rattled on its foundation as Craig killed a person for the first time; he knew he killed him, too.

With all his senses at their peak, he crept to the back door and turned the knob ever so slowly. All remained completely silent as he pushed the door open onto the back pouch. Lightening flashed again, revealing the dead man flung onto the back lawn Craig religiously mowed every weekend. In the instant of light, he saw a red gaping hole where his left eye had once been. His other eye looked back, telling him he was from the Chinese mob. He had just seen them at Gercio's funeral. Maybe Marcella had more control than he thought?

Immediately, Craig ran to the side of the house, hoping they didn't realize they were down a soldier.

•

From her secret crypt in the cellar, Marcella watched The Dragon's assassins encroach Scalici's house. The Looking Spell was working to perfection. In the past, it would peter out when she got to Scalici's home. Tonight, though, tonight would be the night she'd crush the little shit! Then the eye in the page blinked and the image was gone.

"Fuck you! There is no one more powerful than thee! It is Scalici I want to see!" she screamed at the book.

It closed its eye, and remained shut. It shouldn't have done that. It was her own blood flowing in the pages. The flesh on the cover was that of virgins. It was the most powerful book of spells ever penned, and it was hers.

"You need not bother to watch them. My assassins are quite efficient." The Dragon spoke from behind her, still in awe of her power. If she would only continue to let that detective distract her, all that power would be his. For the old dragon had done some homework on witches. "Why don't you hone in on the grandparents, the daughter is probably with them."

"Because he'd kill them before he'd let them have her. Now shut up, old man!" Marcella snarled. "I did not ask you here for your advice."

"Then why am I here?" he asked, reaching for the iron dagger in his

147

sleeve. It had been boiled in the urine of one of her victims. A connection got a sample from Terrell's autopsy.

"I think there is a spell you could help me with." She leaned on the brass music stand her father had given her as a child studying violin. It was beautifully crafted in the shape of a lyre. "This might help me with my power."

Marcella started leafing through the pages to get to the spell. Unseen and unheard, The Dragon slipped the weapon out of his sleeve and into his hand. He had killed many a man in this manner. The witch was powerful, maybe smarter than most, but not smarter than he.

Marcella got to the page she wanted when suddenly the book flipped back to the looking spell. The eye was wide open, showing The Dragon holding a dagger behind her. In that instant her powers were gone, replaced by fear. An explosion blasted her eardrums at the same moment the eye showed the dragon crouching. The old man's body still had enough momentum to send her sprawling forward as it slammed into her. With the dagger still gripped in his hand, the tip buried deep into her fleshy arm.

"Ma'am, are you okay?" Benny's voice called to her from the steps.

"Hell no!" she cried. The dagger was excruciating. "Help me, we don't have time."

Benny rushed to her and pulled the dagger out. Surprising to him, there was no blood. With all her padding, she had extra protection. Without losing a moment's time, Marcella flipped back to the page she was looking for, Cecrops' Spell for Dragons.

"In the Name of Fafnir of the Nibelung horde, I drink the blood of the Dragon Fung of the Blood Triad. Present to me all that is dragon," she invoked, then began to suck the blood out of the old man's wound. She had planned on slicing his neck with a ritual knife, but this would have to do.

Nothing.

She didn't think it would work, but the old man did have the title of The Dragon, and it might have worked in the realm of darkness.

Benny looked on hoping that whatever she was doing would be over soon. For once Marcella was done, he would be second in command.

"Damn it! Don't any of these spells work?" she yelled as the blood streamed down her white bloated cheeks. She then looked to Benny in a rage. "Didn't I tell you to leave us alone?"

"Yes Ma'am, but I didn't trust him with you," Benny answered back without backing down. "Damn good thing I did, too."

"Don't you ever disobey me again!" she hissed, tossing The Dragon's body aside like a beer can.

"Fuck you, ma'am'!" Benny fired back.

Marcella just stared at him.

"I don't care if you roast my balls off or suck my brain out. But if you don't let me watch your back, I'm gonna be dead anyway." He glared back at her, as the blood on her face began to clot and harden.

"So you finally spoke back. It's about time. Okay, I will listen to you next time. And if you do talk to me like that again, I'll do more than roast your balls off."

"Fine. So now that I cleared the air," Benny informed her, "there is someone that concerns me more than Scalici.".

•

Upstairs, Timmy Z kept getting a busy signal as he desperately tried to call Craig.

•

The Chevy was gone as Craig snuck around to the front of the house. It was one person less to worry about, and one less place for them to hide. He looked to the porch where Mrs. McIlvain always sat. They would have to get there to enter the house. All of the windows were on the porch along with the front door. He remained still in hopes of hearing a breath or footstep.

He waited for the next lighting strike. The last one must have hit just down the block, close by, since there was no pause between the flash and the thunder. What he did hear, finally, was the wall of rain coming down the street, hard rain. There was no drizzle or random drops; the rain came down in abrupt turrets. The lightening flashed again. Sure enough, an image of a man was at the far end of the porch. Without yelling police or freeze, Craig just opened fire. His eyes couldn't adjust from the flash quick enough to see, but he heard the man land in the hedges beneath the porch. Seconds later, the thunder clapped like an animal wailing.

Where's the other one?

His eyes returned to him as he squatted under the lawn table. The rain poured over the side, obstructing his view. If he stayed, the other would get him, or get inside the house. He knew he was outside now. Craig ran from under the table, hoping to get a response or see movement. Instead, through the rain, he heard a familiar hum by the driveway. He turned to be bathed in a flash of light. He barely had time to see the figure in the middle holding a gun on him. There was a loud thump, and the light went out.

"What the hell is this crap?" Julie Snow's voice shot out.

With that, the lights came back on. The street lamp showed the last assassin pinned under the front of the car, with Mrs. Snow still in the driver's seat.

"Stay in the car!" Craig yelled to her.

"What's going on?" she cried from the window.

Craig ran to the man she just plowed into. Dressed in black, an automatic pistol was clutched in his hand. The rain continued to pour, washing the blood away from his mouth. From behind, he heard Mrs. Snow scream. She had gotten out of the car against his advice.

"*Oh my god!* That poor man," she bawled.

"That poor man was going to kill us! You're a hell of a shot with that thing." Craig tried to make a joke as he ran back to the porch to make sure the other was just as dead. "Stay right there!" he yelled to her, hoping she'd listen this time.

Inside, Craig switched the lights back on to see the room empty.

"Meredith? Christina?" he called immediately. "It's over!"

Still nothing. He ran to the kitchen to see nothing but the broken window. He darted back to the living room. It was just as silent as the night outside. The closet caught his eye.

"It's okay now. I took care of things," he said to the closet. He marched to the closet door with his gun; he didn't like the fact that no one answered him. He half expected to see blood coming out from under the door. Maybe there were four of them. Pulling the knob, he saw Christina covering Meredith with her body. The popcorn bowl was clenched in her hand.

"Only me!" he assured them, putting the gun back.

Christina looked up to him, her almond shaped eyes wide. "More will come. I don't live far from here."

"Then you're going to get some house guests. You okay, Meredith?" Craig asked, not being able to see her face.

His daughter lifted her face from Christina's side. It was pale, and horribly adult looking. "I'm fine, Daddy. Is Jeannine and her family coming with us?"

Craig had forgotten about them. If Marcella was out to get his family, she might well go after them too. The fact that Mrs. Snow just took out a Chinese assassin might not help their amenity.

"I don't know, hon," he said, looking at Christina.

"They can sleep on the floor," Christina spoke up, still clutching the bowl, ready to bash brains out if called to do so.

"Well let's get going. I'll ask if she wants to come," said Craig, taking his daughter back.

•

After a quick lockup of the house, Craig took them outside where Mrs. Snow had remained. She leaned against her car, pressing her hand against her mouth. Craig had noticed her do this only once before when her cat was found dead in the road two years ago. The rain had stopped as suddenly as it started. Water and dampness seemed to be everywhere.

"Who are they?" she asked, continuing to look down at the man she killed. "Were they sent by someone?"

"Best that you don't know," Craig answered.

"Listen, if my…" She looked up and saw Christina standing behind him.

"Who is this? Is she one of *them?*" Mrs. Snow asked, showing a bit of rage.

"No, they're Chinese. I'm Korean," Christina answered in a not-so-sweet way.

"This is the woman we talked about," Craig explained in his authoritative tone. "I think it's best we stay the night with her. Including you!"

"I'm not leaving my house! What if Jeannine or mother calls? Oh my God! Are they in danger?" she asked, as frenzy began to set in.

"They should be fine, but they may be after you now. Like I said, good shot with the car. You saved my life." Craig tried to get her to lighten up.

"Screw your life! Is my family in danger?" she ranted.

"They shouldn't be. You can call them from Christina's house."

With that, Julie Snow looked Christina dead in the face. "I don't trust you."

Craig shrugged Mrs. Snow's sentiment off and put her and Meredith in his Mustang. They followed Christina's orange Triumph sports car to her house.

Not ten minutes later, the curious viewers that saw Trent's Special found more than they bargained for.

•

Aisha was on the last decade of her Rosary when Chip called.

"Ma, Detective O'Hanlen is on the phone," Ellery's voice boomed out, disrupting her praying.

"I'll get it up here!" she yelled back, wanting only to get back to God, something she had been meaning to do for some time now. With the workload and the kids, her faith had taken a backseat, something she never should have done. She grabbed the phone by the bed where she was kneeling. Chip told her how LeSorbe had disappeared and how a freak tornado did in Trent Gold.

"Were there any others in the building?" she asked about the network building.

"Only the cleaning staff. The rest had gone away for the weekend."

"Chip, this is going to sound crazy, but I think we're all under a curse!" she blurted out, for now there was no doubt in her mind that the devil was now walking amongst them.

"I know." Chip admitted after he drew his breath. "I'm worried about Craig. I've been having nightmares about him and my family."

"So have I." She told him what Timmy Z had told them about Marcella.

"Fucking figures. Can we throw water on her or something?"

"No, Dorothy, but maybe if we exposed her..."

The phone went dead. All she could hear was her own breath in the receiver. She tried to jiggle it, but nothing happened. "ELLERY!" she screamed. "Where are you?"

Never in her life did she want to hear his voice call out to her.

Nothing.

"Good God, Ellery! Don't play with me."

From outside, a role of thunder seemed to mock her. The lights flickered. Aisha grabbed her revolver from the nightstand. Forgetting to let go of her Rosary beads, the two tangled together in her hand. She ran down the stairs, still hoping to see her son sprawled on the floor with that blank look of TV staring. He wasn't there. The lights flickered again, this time staying out a few minutes longer. She yelled throughout the house. "If you hurt him, bitch, I'll ring your fucking head off!"

She went down to the living room, where, ironically, a special report on the TV was showing the wreckage of the network headquarters.

"Apparently no one else was in that part of the building as the tornado hit," the blonde reporter broadcast in her very serious mode.

Aisha paced the floor, waiting for something to happen. The light flickered again with a thunder roll a few minutes later.

"Ellery!" she called again, and the lights went completely out. At first, she worried about not seeing. Yet she could see. Outside, all was dark. The lamps were out inside. *How could she see?* she wondered.

"Reports of severe thunderstorm damage and tornado's are coming in throughout the New York area," the Reporter continued.

Aisha looked at the TV, wondering how it could still be on. Then the picture cut to Chip in his living room dialing the phone.

"Meanwhile, Detective O'Hanlen tried desperately to call detective Barlow back." A voiceover of the reporter spoke in the same type of news tone. The picture cut to Aisha herself in the dark living room, "But her phone line was temporarily out of service."

"Where's my son, you bitch?" she hollered at the screen.

The screen switched to a fire pit. Hundreds of corpses were burning at the stake. Aisha watched in horror as their flesh started to burn away to bone, yet they still seemed to be alive. Their lower jaws still screamed in agony. Shouts of fire spewed from their mouths. The screen then zoomed in to one in particular, Ellery. Before her eyes, she watched her son being burned alive in a ball of flames. Without thinking, she raised her gun and shot the screen.

"Ow, you bitch!" the reporter's voice screamed from the tube.

Sparks flew out the back of the set, but the image on the screen did not go dead. Instead, the reporter came back on screen with a close-up. The bullet hole in the glass was right between her eyes.

"You fucking asshole bitch!" it yelled in Marcella's voice. "Die!"

Aisha suddenly felt as if a car smacked into her. When she was young, she had run into the street after her kick ball. A Buick had hit her and knocked her unconscious. It was the same now as she was thrown back across the room on to the couch. The main force of the blow, though, seemed to go around her. In her hand, she felt something hot. Thinking it was the barrel of her gun at first, she began to realize it was her Rosary beads. On the screen, the infuriated reporter let out a wail that rattled the windows.

"Mom!" Ellery's voice called, piercing the bellowing of the TV.

Aisha knew immediately that this was the real thing. The lights came back on to show the full mess of the living room, smoldering TV and all.

"Are you okay?" he asked, then spotted the TV. "The TV! Oh my God!"

"Where the hell _were_ you?" she asked. His concern for the boob tube was further proof it was indeed her son.

"I went outside to look at the storm coming in. Then it just stopped," he said, as things began to dawn on him. "Were you shooting at someone?"

"No, just the same old crap on TV. Do me a favor and call your dad's precinct, I need him home."

•

Chip's chest froze in place when Aisha's phone died. A part of him felt like it suddenly died, too. Quickly, he tried again and again, his fingers missing the holes in the rotary dial. Each time there would be nothing, not even a busy signal.

Finally a voice answered in the phone company's typical monotone voice. "Sorry, the number you have dialed is temporarily out of service. Please try again."

If Chip had been at Aisha's at the time, he would have realized it was the same voice coming from the TV. His first instincts were to load the family up and drive as far away as possible.

Not at night, too dangerous.

There were forces that were stronger at night. He'd be better off waiting until daylight. He tried Craig again and actually heard a ring at the other end. After the twenty first ring he decided that his buddy probably braved the night and skedaddled for someplace safer. He was sure Craig flipped out when he saw his precious home on TV. He was still contemplating doing the same. What Aisha told him about Marcella was still frightening to him, though he knew it was all true.

He knew what needed to be done was to get the tape from Timmy Z and expose the witch. But if she saw that he was out to get her, she could go after the kids or Barbara, even his folks. So that night, Chip packed up the his family and drove as far from New York as he could with no argument from Barbara at all. Toys were left on the floor and a roast left defrosting in the fridge. It killed him to leave Craig, but family came first.

•

"I don't care young lady! You stay right where you are!" Julie Snow's voice carried on. "Meredith will be fine!"

Craig felt awkward as hell being in Christina's house as his landlord yelled at her daughter.

The house was less than twenty minutes away, overlooking the Great South Bay. It was nowhere as big and aged as the Islip house, yet it too, had a feeling of home. Bookshelves stood in just about every room. Mostly on folklore and worldly cultures, the titles did vary from mathematics to pre-Columbian history. For some reason Craig felt the house should be in the woods of Vermont or Maine instead of the middle of Long Island.

"First thing in the morning, I'm going to Aunt Fanny's to be with Grandma! Don't argue with me!" Julie hollered again, making both Craig and Christina even more uncomfortable. "Stay put, end of story! Love you dear!" She ended sweetly then hung up the phone.

"I'll drive you to your mother's tomorrow, Mrs. Snow." Christina offered, very hesitantly.

"No you won't! I'll call a cab!" she snapped. "And I think I should take Meredith with me," she said to Craig, as if Christina weren't there.

"No, I'm going to send her to her grandparents," Craig said, as if he were admitting defeat.

"But they'll keep her. You know they will!" Julie panicked.

"Better alive with them, than dead with me," Craig sighed. He felt free to talk about Meredith since she went right to sleep in Christina's spare bed the moment they got there.

"Who's behind this? Was it someone from that TV show tonight? I stepped out before the end to check on mother," Julie demanded, with no response at first. "I need to know!"

"They're some of The Dragon's men," Christina answered. "They're part of the Blood Triad from China."

"What's a blood triad?" Craig asked, now enamored with Christina's explanation himself.

"Triads are ancient societies from China. They have been around for centuries, existing in secrecy. They were started by Buddhist monks who hid from the emperors because they were persecuted. Only in the

156

past century have some of them become corrupt and evil."

"Can they take the form of a dragon?" Craig asked.

"I don't think so. I do know of a Celtic spell that can transform someone if they drink the blood of a dragon." Christina walked over to one of the bookshelves. "I have literature that discusses it, but not the spell itself. Most of the works I have use dragons as parables."

"What?" Julie asked, actually showing some interest herself.

"In both Asian and European texts, dragons are sometimes representative of the choices we make, whereas wolves do not make choices on their own and go along with the pack. Dragons are solitary creatures that will make a choice different than the rest. With every decision, you either fly as a dragon or run with the wolves," she explained to them as she studied the titles of her books.

"Daddy!" Meredith's voice called out.

"I'll go to her. You two can go on with your dragon crapola." Julie headed toward the sound of Meredith's voice.

"Mrs. Snow," Craig called to her as she started to leave, "Thank you. I love you and your family very much."

Julie stopped and turned back with a tear in her eye. "Don't go faggot on me now, Detective." She sobbed, then went off with Meredith.

"Your mother's jealous of me," Christina whispered.

"My mother's dead," Craig said without paying too much attention.

"I mean her, she thinks of you as her son," Christina corrected.

Craig turned to her. "And what do you think of me? Tell me the truth."

Christina sat on her sofa and bowed her head. "I've told you about my dreams."

"Not what they were about."

"You. They have been of you. I first dreamt of you when I first entered adolescence. I could not see your face, but it was you. When I married my husband, I knew it would not work, for he was not you," she explained. "Lately the dreams have been explicit, extremely explicit. I know every scar and birthmark on your body, even the burn mark on your thigh."

As a child, Craig had tried to make his dad a cup of coffee to sober him up. Barely able to reach the stove, the hot kettle fell off and burned his left inner thigh.

"*Are* you a witch?" Craig asked, repeating Aisha's initial question.

"I don't know anymore. All I know is that I am meant to be with you. Our time has come and we would be together."

Craig remembered the first woman he fantasized for, Angelique, the witch from 1960's horror soap opera, *Dark Shadows*. It was the first woman he ever had a hard-on for. Now the same feeling was here, uncontrollable and overwhelming.

"I've dreamed of you also. Just the other night..."

The mood was suddenly halted with a phone ringing. Both of them gasped as if cold water had been tossed on them.

"Who could that be?" Craig quickly asked.

"Beats me. Everyone knows I'm in bed by now."

"Answer it, but pretend they woke you up."

She let it ring a few more times, then answered. "Um, hello," she said in a groggy voice.

"Put that partner of mine on now!" Aisha commanded.

"Detective Barlow?" Christina answered. Craig immediately swiped the phone from her.

"Aisha?" Craig asked.

"It ain't Christy Love, sucker. What's going on?" she demanded.

"Some blood tripod tried to whack us at the house. How did you know I was here?" he asked, as Christina smirked at his mispronunciation.

"Remember, I use bitchcraft. I saw how you two were eyeing each other. Fortunately, she's listed in the book and you're lucky Marcella doesn't know about her. I sent a squad car by your house and they found your dinner guests. Everyone all right?"

"Everyone's fine. Mrs. Snow is with us. We have got to get to Timmy Z."

"Well good luck! Chip took his family and skipped town. I'm tempted to do the same with my kids tomorrow."

Craig protested, "No, we need to get inside Marcella's house. Once we're in, we can get Timmy Z into protective custody."

"Do I look like Dorothy to you, Mr. Wizard?" She was pissed off. "I saw an image of my son being burned alive tonight. Then witchy-poo tried to kill me! If I didn't have Jesus and Mary with me, Albequrk would be autopsying *me* right now!"

"If we don't expose her with that tape, she'll get even stronger. Then where are ya gonna go? Answer me that?" Craig yelled back. "The way to stop her is right there! Don't forget we promised to help the guy!"

"Don't you yell at me! I've been there for you too often. Sorry, once my family is safe, then maybe I'll help. Maybe!" She was more upset than mad. "And Timmy Z is in no danger now. He's the apple of her eye again."

"Not if she finds that tape!" Then he thought about what she said. She didn't deserve his wrath, and who was he to endanger her family? "Sorry again. Good luck, partner. Take care of yourself."

"You too, I have feeling we'll be back together real soon," she said, openly crying out loud.

"Don't go lesbian on me now!" he scolded.

"*What!*" she screamed.

"You know what I mean," he tried to cover.

"No I don't! You better lay off that Saki she's giving you, boy!" she teased.

"I will, master," he kidded back, in a way he usually didn't.

She didn't say goodbye, instead she just hung up.

"What's going on?" Christina asked.

"Marcella, she's going after our families now." He pushed the receiver down, but didn't hang up.

"I heard you say you could expose her. That would weaken her powers." She perked up. "Dark magic is just as it states, it's dark. If you throw light into darkness, it goes away."

Craig picked up the phone and started dialing.

"Who are you calling?" Christina asked.

"My father-in-law. I've got to arrange a few things," he said, suddenly very intent and focused.

Chapter 11

DRAGON DREAMS

In her dream that night, Meredith was flying again. Her arms spread apart like an eagle as she soared far above the city. Before she knew it, she was above her grandparents and Fire Island. Although the island was no more than a string of land, she could see every last detail, down to grandma's bird feeder in the back yard. She could still see the lights of the holiday traffic driving out to the far edge of Long Island, every car coming into perfect focus. Out in the ocean, she saw whales diving deep in the water after small schools of fish. Looking north, she saw the coast of Connecticut and decided to fly toward it.

Within minutes, she was over Hartford, then New Haven. She and her father were there last November on a vacation. One day they decided to go to Cranberry Farms to go horseback riding. Excitement had filled her heart when they drove up the road to all the barns at the farm. Unfortunately, there were no horses. A big sign on the gate told them they had moved to a new set of stables. Excitement filled her again as they made their way back to the road to the "New" Cranberry Farms. The pamphlet at the bed and breakfast they stayed in showed all the beautiful horses with their long running manes galloping through the fields. It took her dad awhile, after getting lost a couple times, but finally they reached the big red barn with Cranberry Farms painted in big white letters on the top. She could see the horses sticking their heads out the side. In the back, the hills were speckled with all the different colors autumn could provide.

"Goddamn it!" her dad said—and he never spoke like that, except when Uncle Chip was over to drink beer. "They must have their head up their asses."

Like the other gate, this one too, had a sign which read: "Sorry, we are not open to the public yet. Please come back and see us soon."

"What type of crap is that? When's soon?" her dad yelled.

The whole weekend was miserable and the sign was all she remembered. So she decided to take them up on her offer and go back.

Whoosssssh.

She flew to the big red barn. Yet all the horses were jumping up and down in their windows, some trying to get out. From the house, people in their pajamas were running to the barn.

She didn't see it when she first got there, but now she could see a big hole in the roof. Inside she saw something familiar, an owl pellet.

•

Craig spent an hour on the phone with his ex-father-in-law. Once everything was settled and in place, the feeling of calmness had returned. Christina had waited patiently and in the same position since Aisha called. She *was* beautiful. She reached out her hand and he took it willingly.

"This is meant to be. We are meant to be together," she said gently.

"I know." He knew they would be intimate in a few moments. He also knew that a child would be conceived from their union that very moment. He just prayed that Meredith and Mrs. Snow stayed asleep.

•

The lovemaking was tender. Every touch seemed to seduce each other into their spells even more. After it was done, sleep came fast.

•

Craig was flying, naked and alone. He was flying over Connecticut where he had taken Meredith the year before. In the sky in front of him, all the stars seemed to disappear. Some of them came back into view as others suddenly went out.

It was the dragon.

It flew and flipped in the air like a dolphin frolicking in water. Beneath it was Cranberry Farms, where the idiots ruined what would have been a perfect weekend for the two of them. There was plenty to do while they were up there, but Meredith wanted to see the horses so bad. Even if she could have just petted them it would have been fine. But no, the dumb fucks couldn't have put it in the pamphlets that they had moved and wouldn't be open for months. Rage now boiled in his stomach. He just about forgot about the beast in front of him when it stopped in mid-air and arched its head up.

Oh God, it saw me!

He looked down and saw he was miles above the ground. With a snap, he looked back to the dragon. It had reared its long neck back far in the air.

It's heaving, Craig recognized.

Sure enough, the dragon thrust its head forward and expelled a large mass of fur and bones, like the one that contained Gercio. The horses below screamed as the mass fell into the barn. It landed square in the middle, between the rows of stables, missing the horses Meredith cared so much for. It was full of leg bones and cattle skulls. Craig looked back at the monster; terrified to see its orange eyes staring back had him.

Oh, crap!

In mid-air Craig turned around and flew away. He somehow willed himself forward at the speed of a sonic jet. He looked back to see the dragon flying closer. Every time it flapped its wings, he could see the intricate weave of veins coursing through the skin. He could see them pulsating as it brought up its immense claws, like a hawk readying to snatch a rat. The air around him swirled and bobbed him around in the turbulence.

The great talons grabbed him tight. One of their sharp edges sliced his side open. He could feel his own blood squirt over his stomach as the dragon started flying straight up. Higher and higher they rose, until it suddenly dropped him. The release from the claw was a great relief; he didn't care if he was falling to his death. He was free.

Out of nowhere he was grabbed again. This time not by a dragon's claw, but by a woman. She wrapped herself around him as they both plummeted down to Earth. Her body was soft and her wildly blowing hair enveloped his head so he couldn't see her face. Her nipples were hard, pressed deep between his ribs.

He liked it.

Before he knew it, he was inside her. They began to tumble head over heels as he thrust himself. Each time a feminine moan of ecstasy came from within the mass of hair. He knew he was close to the ground but did not care, the intensity was too great. As their descent accelerated, he released himself. It was hot. Her body froze; he could feel every muscle contract as she arched her back.

They were falling faster now and the woman let him go and flew away. To his terror, he saw the ground less than a mile away from him. He tried to will himself away but he continued to fall. Roads and pathways throughout the forest came into focus to the last detail. Closer and closer the woods came, 'til he saw the roof of a great estate. Every shingle was clear to him now as he tried to regain control, but couldn't.

•

Craig screamed into wakefulness. Something he had never done. He was hoping the whole ordeal was a dream and he'd be at home. This lasted a whole two seconds until he oriented himself and realized he was in Christina's bed, with her nestled in his shoulder. His life had permanently changed and the existence he had was now gone. The first rays of the morning were shining through the blinds to show Christina's delicate face. He was scared, not of Marcella, but of the life that was now ahead of him. Would Marcella harm Meredith or Christina? Was Marcella the dragon? He might not ever see Chip, Aisha, or the Snows ever again. Looking down at his future, he went to brush her hair away from her face.

What he saw shocked him. His hand was caked in dried blood. Immediately he looked down to his side of the bed and found the sheets were stained red with his blood. He pulled the sheet away to see a two foot long clotted gash in his side, right where the dragon's claw slashed him in his dream.

•

Aisha had packed in a whirlwind the night before. Germaine had made it home in record time. She kept forgetting she had a loving husband and took him for granted. Maybe Craig was right in that she should have put her family above all else. Then again, Craig only had one daughter; she had four sons and a husband. Potential shootouts would have been more relaxing sometimes. Also, unlike her partner, her family didn't need her as much. They all loved each other, but they were all leaving the nest. Germaine was just as busy as she was, and was just as content to go fishing whenever he wanted. She also knew that he would give it all up in a second if she needed him.

After twenty years of marriage, she knew him well. He'd tell the boys at work that she was "reeling in the line" and putting her foot down. Her detective eyes and ears had let her know he did this just to spend more time with her and save face with the men pack. He did not like her working on the Gercio case, yet did not stand her way. All she had to do was tell him that Marcella's men were watching the house and he helped pack immediately. She omitted the witchcraft portion of the story. Germaine was smart, he was not going to have a showdown in the middle of a residential neighborhood, especially after Craig's.

They were off to his cousin's hunting cabin in Oneonta, and were going to hunker down until things passed. He ran to the store to get supplies for the cabin, with three of the kids, as Ellery packed the rest of his stuff.

"Ma, can you please tell me what's going on? Are we in danger?" Ellery shouted from his room.

"No, it's a vacation! What do you *think?*" she quipped back, thinking that she should have answered more delicately.

"Then people are after us, cool!" he answered with elation.

There was a rapid knock on the door, a desperate knock.

"Don't get that!" she yelled out to Ellery.

She heard her son go immediately silent. It became suddenly real to him.

"Stay in your room until I call for you," she instructed, then looked out the window.

In the street below she saw a sedan, the type a cop would drive. With her revolver, she crept down the steps as the rapping banged again. From a window at the base of the steps, she looked out to her guest and was utterly floored. It was Devaney. He looked haggard and his shoulders were slumped forward.

"Barlow! I need your help! Please!" he called out.

Despite what an asshole the man was, Aisha could never turn her back to someone genuinely in need.

Damn it!

She went to the door and slowly opened it. Before saying a word, she scanned the yard and street for anything out of the ordinary then she looked to Devaney. Streaks of gray hair sprouted out of his head, like Petey in the alley. His face looked like it aged thirty years.

"My God, what happened?" she asked, letting him into the house.

"I wish I knew," he answered, entering the living room. He immediately looked at the shot-up TV. "But it looks like you've had something similar."

"How much do you know?" she asked as the man teetered.

"We've unleashed something evil." he said, collapsing on the couch.

"Who's *we?*" she asked, her mind beginning to put more pieces together.

"I've been giving information to Trent Gold," he confessed. "He wanted information on Craig to humiliate him. He thought he could play out this supernatural angle. It looked liked he was right, and shit's been happenin' to me ever since."

She didn't bother asking him what had been happening to him, she could only imagine.

"What brings you to me? How can I help you?" she asked, wondering if she could get Ellery's and her own ass out soon.

"My daughter. I need you to pick up my wife and daughter. I'm afraid if I go near them, or I'll bring whatever evil there is to them." He took her hand.

"And what makes you think I won't?"

"I think your soul is better at fighting evil than mine." He smirked. "You were able to fight her off already."

Damn it!

"Where are they?" she asked with reservation.

Devaney's face lit up. "I told them to wait at the Delphi Diner. It's right around the corner and they should be there right now. I can't go near them!" He said it, looking around as if he was being watched. "Take them with you or just get them the hell away from here."

"Alright," Aisha agreed, "but one thing."

"What?" he asked.

She slapped him across the face, hard enough to send some blood splattering on her beautiful couch.

"You're still a racist pig! And don't think for a moment I'll forget or forgive what you said to me!"

Looking down, he muttered, "I wouldn't expect you to."

•

True to her word, Mrs. Snow took a taxi at dawn. She asked if she could take Meredith with her for safety, and again Craig turned her down. Shortly after, Craig and Christina met Sandra at the ferry.

"Where's grandpa?" the child asked her grandmother.

"Business dear," Sandra replied, then turned to the others. "Are you two going to be okay?"

"I hope so, Mom," Craig answered without saying any more.

Meredith, still sleepy, nodded off in her grandmother's arms as they went back on the ferry. Craig and Christina waited till the ferry was well out of the canal before they went back to the car.

"You'll be with her again," Christina said. "I can see it."

"I hope so," he nodded, taking her hand and kissing it.

"There's something else," she replied.

"I know. You're pregnant," he smiled. "Now there are more people on my list to worry about."

She didn't know why, but his knowing did not come as a surprise to her. The bond between them must be getting stronger.

"What are you going to do now?" she asked, already knowing the answer.

"You've seen the movie. Only this time it's a tape and not a broom-stick I must retrieve."

"I know you'll say no, but can I come with you?"

"You're right, no."

"I can see things. If she uses her magic, I might be able to help."

"I'm not an expert, but I can tell her magic does not work on me. I'd be worm meat by now if it did." He opened the door for her.

"She's growing stronger. Whatever is blocking her from you may not hold out for much longer."

"Well, maybe you can help. Can you become a dragon and kill her?" he asked in interrogation mode.

"I'm not the dragon! I told you! The dream you had last night was just a dream. If I could have done so, I would have protected you if I were the dragon." She started to cry.

"Listen, I can tell we were driven together by some force." He said firmly, "And, yes, I was in love with you after meeting you once. That does not mean I know you. I don't know what you're like or what you're capable of. And don't forget, you lied to me."

"I never *lied* to you!" she cried. Above them, the seagulls seemed to have echoed her scream.

"You weren't completely honest with me at first. That's lying in my book," he said going to his side of the car.

"Do you think I mauled you in your sleep, or did you do it yourself?" she asked. "Maybe you're the dragon? Deep in your subconscious maybe?"

"One flaw with that, the dragon's a skirt. Female."

"Should I leave you then? Go far away and have our baby alone?" she asked.

"If that's what you want. I'd rather you'd stayed. Let me get to know you better and vice versa." He climbed into the driver's seat.

Christina had no idea what to do next. So she got in beside him and could only think of one thing to say. "You're a very strange man."

"I know, that's why you love me," he grinned, taking her hand. "And no...you can't come with me. Please stay at home."

•

"For the last time, you're off the mark," Marcella said to Benny. From the attic window she looked at her husband and son planting a tree in front of the house.

Benny bit his bottom lip. "He's scared, I can see it in his eyes. I've seen how finks look before they squeal."

"You saw how he stuck up for me! Is that someone who's afraid?" she asked, pointing to him out the window. "He's had plenty of opportunities to leave."

"And he knows that you'd eventually get him," Benny retorted.

"The only persons that could be of any harm to me are being taken care of by my spells."

"Not all your spells are working. Some are still alive," he reminded her.

"Even if they are, they'll all running away. That's just as good. The ones that stay, you can deal with. Rosary beads are not going to stop your gunners," she said with confidence.

"Then let me do my job. Timmy is plotting against you."

"Wrong, wrong, *wrong*!" she scowled.

"Hey, love blinds people."

"And what do you know about love, Benny? Ever loved any of the women you've been with? How many kids have you fathered? Do you even care what becomes of them?" For a moment she almost sounded human.

"No. And it's better that I don't," he said honestly, and she agreed.

"Alright," she relented, "I'll keep an eye on him. If you suspect anything more, you tell me and no one else."

"Yes ma'am."

•

Outside, Timmy Z and his son placed an oak sapling into the hole they dug together. To his inner thigh, he had taped the cassette of his wife's confession.

"Georgy," Timmy whispered.

"Yeah, Dad?" Georgy replied shoving a pile of mud back in the hole.

"Don't forget, when we go and hide on mommy, you can't talk," he said, resisting the urge to look up and see if anyone was watching. He knew Benny was onto him and he couldn't act suspicious. It was odd that he was depending on Marcella to protect him. If Benny had his way, he'd be planted in a foundation somewhere.

"I won't, Dad. It'll spoil the game," Georgy whispered back, giggling.

•

It was 10:30 AM when Jeannine made it to the Messinal's beach house. These people had no idea what they were up against, and she was ready to let them know. The cedar shake house was not as big as she thought it would be, considering how much money there was involved. A brass bell hung in front of a screened in porch filled with wicker furniture. Jeannine began to think that maybe Meredith might grow to like it here with these people, and forget about her and real family. With her blue eyes and ponytail, Jeannine fit in like a glove, to the na-

169

tives. She could even get to like this place herself. Grabbing the rope, she gave the bell a ring and within moments a maid came to the porch.

"Good morning. Are you here to see the lady of the house?" the maid asked.

"No, I'm Jeannine, Meredith's babysitter. I was worried about her." She watched the woman's face contract into a worried look.

"Who is it, Hanna?" Sandra's voice called out.

"Can you come here, ma'am, I think you should talk to this young lady," Hanna called back, not taking her eyes off Jeannine.

Sandra came to the door, but would not step on the porch. Jeannine could see her white tennis dress but not her face.

"How may I help you, dear?" Sandra asked, staying back in the shadows.

"I'm Jeannine. Meredith lives with me and my family." Jeannine tried to sound friendly. "I'd like to see how's she's doing. I'm a little frightened for her."

"I'm sorry dear, but my husband took her to work with him today," Sandra said smiling. Jeannine could see the white teeth appear like the cat from Alice in Wonderland.

"I thought he retired," Jeannine came back quickly.

"He still owns it, dear. Why don't you come back—"

"Jeannine!" Meredith's voice yelled out. Like a puppy dog, she came running out of the house and flew through the porch door.

"Hey kid!" Jeannine laughed and grabbed the girl up into her arms.

"Where have you been?" Meredith asked.

"Oh, you know my mom. She had me stay with friends." Jeannine grabbed Meredith's nose between her fingers.

"You must be Mrs. Snow's daughter," Sandra acknowledged. "Please come in, before you're seen."

With Meredith in her arms, Sandra, who looked around for anyone else out of the ordinary, ushered Jeannine in.

"I'm sorry about what happened at your house," Sandra said.

"At least Meredith's safe. Right Meredith?"

"Now that you're here." Meredith answered, then turned to Sandra and Hanna. "She's like a cazillionth degree black belt."

"That's nice dear, now let's get inside," Sandra added, growing more impatient.

•

After her third piece of chocolate pecan pie and fourth glass of milk, Jeannine finally called it quits for food.

"Are you sure you're full, hon?" Hanna asked the teen.

"Oh my God, yes!" Jeannine answered holding her mouth.

Seated at the table with her, Sandra poured another cup of coffee.

"In the old days, this would be a Bloody Mary," Sandra informed them, looking at the two girls making faces at each other. "Meredith, why don't you go find the Monopoly game? We could play a few games together."

"Okay, Grandma," Meredith answered and ran off.

"Tell me, Jeannine, are you eighteen yet?" Sandra sipped her coffee.

"No, I'm only sixteen. I start my senior year next week," she said, checking out the pure white kitchen. It looked like a time capsule from the 1930's.

"How would you like to spend the next year studying abroad?" Sandra asked again, then immediately looked down to her coffee cup.

"Excuse me?" Jeannine asked.

"If, God forbid, anything happened to her father, we'd be left to raise her. Would you consider being an au-pare?" Sandra asked her.

"A what?"

"A full-time mother's helper, dear."

"Why, do you think something will happen to Mr. Scalici?" Jeannine asked.

"You saw what happened last night. I'm almost tempted to take Meredith now and run off to Europe. Even here I feel it's dangerous," Sandra confided.

"Who's after him? Maybe we can go to the news people?" Jeannine asked.

"I don't know, but they killed my daughter!" Sandra snapped bitterly as she poured another cup of coffee.

"Maybe not. I mean, why her and not us? Craig really didn't have a strong bond to her anymore." Jeannine looked back for Meredith.

"Well, if anything happens to Craig, I would pay you to help raise Meredith. I didn't do such a good job the first time." Sandra added, "Don't get me wrong, I want her to be with her father. I'm just afraid we're going to lose him too."

"We'll see what my mother says." Jeannine felt a sudden chill.

•

A brown Caprice Classic was the only car parked in the diner's parking lot. Aisha didn't like this. In all the commotion, she forgot the place was closed a few days for renovations. Being a holiday, none of the workers were there. Just as she was about to back out of the lot, a woman's head popped up from around the far corner of the building. Wrapped in a kerchief and sunglasses, she looked like a poor Jackie O impersonation. No doubt she wanted a secret password. With that, she flashed her headlights figuring she would get the hint. She did. She saw her turn her head to talk to someone. The daughter no doubt.

God, what type of family could Devaney have spawned?

She watched as she tried to get the girl to come out from hiding. It looked like a bad comic sketch, with the mother trying to get the girl to listen. Aisha knew all too well what it was like to get children to listen to you. Finally, Mrs. Devaney waved Aisha to drive down to them. She looked around and saw nothing but normal traffic passing by. She clutched her Rosary a little harder, just in case, and drove to the frantic mother and daughter. They already drove Marcella off once.

Aisha slammed on the brakes. How did Devaney know she drove Marcella off? The woman by the diner stopped, and said something to the other behind the building. Aisha threw the car in reverse and raced back the way she came. Just then, Devaney pulled up and blocked the exit with a long LTD. Again she stopped. In front of her, the woman was pulling a gun with a silencer from under her clothes. Palumbo's two goons, the ones Craig caught casing his house, both appeared beside her with silencer guns.

172

Great!

The choice was an easy one. She floored the car in reverse and rammed Devaney's LTD broad side. She had a small satisfaction seeing the son of a bitch throw his hands up as if they were going to stop her car at full speed. The force of the blow sent the car half way into the street, but not enough to get it out of the way. There was the short sound of glass breaking and her windshield suddenly became a spider web of bullet holes and cracks. She threw the car into drive and floored it. As if still being a prick, Devaney's car would not let go of rear bumper. Bullets still pelted the car as she sunk below the dash. She kept her foot on the gas, then felt the car lurch, then break free. The smell of burning rubber filled the car as she raced towards the three gunmen.

She didn't dare pick her head up to look and hoped she was heading in the right direction. There was a quick thud and the windshield crashed in along with the body of one of the men. The car then spun around as if someone grabbed the side of it. With something to shield her from bullets now, she poked her head up over the wedged-in thug. She had clipped the side of the diner and the others had dived behind the building.

Before they could get up, she threw the car in reverse again and charged the other car like a bull going after a matador. She hit the car with full force while more bullets hit the car and the body blocking her. Throwing the car in drive, she gunned it back up to where Devaney's smashed LTD still blocked her escape. She heard the bullets shooting out the back windshield as she gained speed.

Devaney raised his bloody face up just as Aisha bore down on him. This time he only had time to open his mouth as she plowed into him. The goon stuck in the windshield was launched across both cars, into the street where traffic now came to a screeching halt. Shoving the car far enough, Aisha squeezed the car out of the lot as more bullets raced by her ear. Almost thinking she wouldn't make it, she finally made it to the street. With one last look, she saw Devaney had also been catapulted into the street, through the side window. His luckless body had made the mistake of landing right in her way.

Oh well.

173

Without hesitation, she ran him right over and made her escape. She made it two blocks before she realized she had two slugs in her side.

•

"Oh no, I've been shot!" Meredith yelled grabbing her side. She had just landed on Reading Railroad and was set to buy it.

Both Jeannine and Sandra grabbed for her, but it was Jeannine that got her. They immediately looked at her side to find nothing but pure white skin.

"Where? Where are you shot?" Jeannine cried.

"My side! Are you goddamned blind?" she yelled in Aisha's voice.

Again the women looked to find nothing. And just as suddenly, Meredith looked up to the two caregivers.

"What happened?" she asked.

Behind them, Hanna watched and spoke to herself, "Lord save us, the evil is near."

Chapter 12

RESCUE FROM WITCH MANSION

This would make a good TV show, Craig thought.

Up until the past few days, police work was nothing like TV. Once in awhile Craig did fantasize about having his own TV show. Hell, they had one about a big fat slob and a geezer older than most giant redwoods. It always amazed him how they could slug it out with four or five bad guys twice their size and still win. For crying out loud, Meredith could kick the crap out of both of them. He did fit the bill for a cop show—young, black partner, beautiful girlfriend, cool car (although you don't use it for work), and a salty landlady. Then reality came back to him, his TV life was fading fast. Timmy Z held the only possible key that might get it back.

From the Texaco gas station before Marcella's exit, he looked to the hill where Alder Lake was and her mansion stood. Of all the thoughts going through his head, the thought of Aisha's Dorothy comment was ringing the loudest. Actually, he couldn't get her out of his mind and his side was started to have sharp pains. At first he thought it was stomach cramps—his last meal was popcorn—then he started thinking appendicitis.

What the fuck? I'll probably be dead in an hour any way.

Craig took the Mustang up into the Catskills, trying to figure out how to sneak into Marcella's compound. Considering he had never been to the place, winging it was his only option. The road banked and dipped like a roller coaster, with mountains on one side and sheer drops on the other. All of it was breathtakingly beautiful, and somewhat familiar. Like seeing Christina at the college, he had seen this place before in his dreams. Each turn and offshoot were clear to him, he had seen it all like a map when he was falling from the sky.

The roof.

It then came to him: the roof in his dream was Marcella's mansion. When the road widened a bit, he pulled over and closed his eyes. Slowing, the image of the area came back to him. With the mansion in the middle there was only one road to the house. On the other side though, what looked liked a footpath ended about a quarter mile behind the house. Judging by the thick overgrowth, it looked like it was purposely closed off years ago. Since Marcella was not one for taking long walks, odds were they didn't even know it was there.

Craig had his plan.

•

The old path wound through the hillside, unscathed from any human debris. Clear skies and lush green trees along the way gave Craig a feeling of euphoria. His head felt as if it was swimming in the nature around him. What a wonderful place to bring his growing family. It seemed so pure; that he felt it should have rejected Marcella like a healthy body rejects an infection. She was unnatural and not meant to be. There should have been something to counteract her, to balance the whole mess out. He was convinced more than ever that she was the dragon. Why she couldn't be one all the time was still a mystery.

The rocks of the narrow path were well-packed. For how many hundreds of years people had used it, it was as good as pavement. His sneakers didn't even make a sound in all the wonderful silence. Part of him felt like a Jack Frost poem, and while he wanted to stop and admire the woods, the same part told him that he would be very acquainted with these woods.

In the meantime, the pain in side began to feel like cuts. They didn't hurt him, but he could have sworn he was being cut. In the end of the dream the night before, the gash he got from the dragon hurt. It still ached a bit.

Before he knew it, he was in a clearing that overlooked Marcella's. The house was beautiful. It had more taste than she was capable of, right down to the weathervane on the chimney, a tall brass ship gleaming in the sun. Below it was just what he wanted to see, Timmy Z and his son out in front. Now it was just a matter of getting them out.

•

Craig had noticed four well-dressed guards in the area of the house. He was sure there were more that couldn't be seen. The four-car garage appeared to be unwatched. As Craig figured it, security was probably lax. With all of her competition now either with her or dead, the idea of a hit would be non-existent. The men on duty would be watching the driveway and the road below.

He saw something—the tool shed. If he could get to Tim, then maybe he could get Marcella to give him a hand. Wouldn't that be a kick in the ass.

•

Georgy was patting down the last of the mud around the tree when his father told him to go rinse off with the hose. The last thing he wanted to do was get his mother mad. Tim collected the shovels and brought them back to the tool shed. It was just out of view from the upper windows, so Tim loved going to it just to drive whoever was watching nuts. Sometimes he would just stay there and straighten up the tools until ol' Benny would come to check him out.

"How big do you think it will get, Dad?" Georgy asked while washing the mud off his hands.

"As big as the house some day," Tim answered with a smile. *God, I have to get him out of here!*

He opened the shed door to see Craig standing inside.

"Need a hoe?" Craig asked, holding the gardening tool.

"Are you crazy?" Timmy Z whined, perspiration immediately breaking out on his forehead.

"Why, yes, yes I am. Step into my office," Craig said with a straight face. "We have a plan to hatch."

●

Just as Timmy thought, Benny had been keeping a sharp eye on him. In Benny's eyes, Timmy was too much of a wimp to try anything blatant, but he would try to sneak away if he had the chance. It pissed him off that he went back to the tool shed again. He knew he did it on purpose, and as soon as Marcella saw the light, he would personally kick his face in. Waiting patiently, he saw Timmy emerge with the normal glib smile just to tick him off more. This time though, the little dick looked right at him and gave him the finger.

That Fuck!

As the kid continued to wash off, Benny watched Timmy march on to the porch. Just as he went out of sight, Benny heard the front door slam shut.

"Marcella! Get down here now!" Timmy Z's voice exploded.

Simultaneously, Benny heard Marcella thundering down the attic steps. She was going to rip him a new asshole. He had to see this. Timmy was standing in the middle of the floor as Marcella descended the grand staircase. At the banister, Benny looked on with delight.

"Who do you think you're talking to?" Marcella snorted.

"My goddamn wife! That's who! Start treating me as your husband or fry me! I'm tired of that Benny shithead watching me and pawing you!" Timmy yelled at her.

"You Fuck!" Benny yelled from the top of the top of the stairs. He knew exactly what the little shit was doing. He just did it to her the other night himself. "Don't listen to him!"

Confused, Marcella looked to the two men on either side of her. "What the hell is going on?"

"That turd has been watching my every move and every crap I take! He wants me out of the way so he can have you himself!" Timmy continued.

"That's a lie! I told you not to trust him!" Benny countered.

"So you have been telling her shit!" Timmy raved. "Keep your hands off my wife, buddy!"

"Timmy, are you jealous?" Marcella asked completely stunned.

"Of course I'm jealous! Who wouldn't be?" Timmy added.

Benny realized he was in big trouble.

●

The next obstacle in Craig's way was the guard in the garage. This part of the plan had to be delicate and silent. Without a silencer, he couldn't shoot the guy. A karate chop that instantly knocked someone out only happened on TV. So Craig could only hope for his famous luck to help him out.

Peering in the rear window, he saw the guard seated on the hood of Marcella's limo. With a Desert Eagle gun in a shoulder holster and shoulder-length hair, he looked like a rock star meets the Godfather. The place was too quiet to even open the window. He sat and prayed that something opportune would happen—and it did. The front door opened and a young maid in pumps walked in.

"Anna baby," the guard eagerly greeted the maid.

"I took an early break, Joey. So why don't you take me for a ride?" she flirted.

"But you're such a prude," Joey teased.

She walked to him and pulled down her top. "I need you to check my headlights."

Feeling like he'd just stepped into a porno flick, Craig watched, almost feeling guilty. As the couple started going at it full throttle, he opened the window and snuck to the Mercedes coupe. At the pace the two were going, Craig was tempted to walk out and start doing jumping jacks just to see if they noticed.

•

"You don't think I've seen you eyeballing her?" Timmy yelled.

"Don't listen to him, 'ma'am!" Benny protested. "Why would I even..." Benny quickly changed his argument, "...try to take her away from you."

"So the thought *has* crossed your mind!" Timmy concluded, with Marcella falling for the whole shebang.

Benny knew Timmy had the upper hand. He also knew that he would never have thought of this himself.

"I need my space! I'm going for a walk and I don't want loverboy here eyeing me! I don't trust him!" Timmy proclaimed and marched back out the door.

Benny wanted to follow and see what he was up to, but that was a certain death warrant for himself. Any argument at this point could easily be taken the wrong way by her.

"Ma'am, he's distracting you," he said calmly.

"I want you to back off from him. He's right, you've been up his ass ever since I got him back," she snapped, teetering on explosion.

"Alright. I'll back off. I just have your best interest in mind."

"Do you?" Marcella smiled.

The thought of being romantic with her flew through his mind, followed by a wave of nausea. "So, do me a favor then. Keep an eye on him yourself. He has nothing to hide from you."

•

Heart racing, Tim looked around for his son from the porch. Since there were no gunshots, he figured Scalici made it to the garage. All he had to do now was find his son. Calling for him was no good, Marcella would wonder why. He walked over to the tree they just planted and saw him admiring it.

How much of Marcella's craft had his son inherited? Just then, Georgy looked up to his dad and gave him a big smile. The last thing he wanted to do was to take the child away from his mother. It was just something that had to be done. And if things continued as they were going, he should be off to Israel within an hour.

"Daddy, can we plant another one?" Georgy asked.

Bingo!

"Of course we can! Let's go into town and buy one!" Timmy Z yelled loud enough for them to hear; nothing suspicious about buying a tree. If he moved quickly enough, Benny wouldn't have time to send his goons.

Georgy jumped to his feet and ran to the garage.

"Don't run!" Timmy Z shouted as if all was normal.

•

Craig waited patiently and started to let the air out of all the tires as the guard and maid started to climax. Now he encountered another threat—wanting to laugh. Lord knows how many guns were walking around ready to kill him, along with the evil mob witch. With all that, all he wanted to do was laugh at the situation he was in. When the door opened and the little kid just stood and watched, Craig lost it and snorted. The guard jerked his head up and went for his gun. Panic filled his face as he saw Georgy standing there.

"Fuck!" he gasped, and quickly tucked everything back in.

"What's wrong?" the disappointed maid asked, then saw Georgy and screamed.

Tim came to the door and quickly covered Georgy's eyes.

"What the hell are you two doing?" Tim screamed.

"They're wrestling, Dad." Georgy answered from under his hand.

"Mr. Z, I'm so sorry," the guard apologized. "Please don't tell your wife."

The maid finished gathering herself up and ran out the door.

"Get out of here! We'll talk later!" Tim glared at the guard.

"Yes, sir," the guard whimpered and left the building.

The roar of Craig's laughter then filled the room. "Wrestling, that's good."

"This isn't funny! Can we get out of here?" Tim responded without amusement.

Georgy looked to Craig and recognized him immediately. "It's the cop from TV! Is he a friend of yours?" Georgy asked wide-eyed.

"Yes, he's your friend too," Tim answered.

Craig walked to Georgy, knelt down to eye level, and smiled. "Now Georgy, I need you to listen to me. We're going to play a little game of hide and seek. Your mother is going to love it."

"Mom doesn't like playing games," Georgy said as his smile began to disappear.

"Oh, she'll like this one. Now it's very important that you stay very quiet and do exactly what we say." Craig stuck out his hand and spat into it. "Deal?"

Georgy stuck out his hand and did the same. "Deal!"

They shook on it. That's when Craig felt as if two cold plates were touching him, one over his right chest and the other on his low left rib cage. A jolt connected the two points within his body and threw Craig back into the limo. For a moment he could not breath or even move.

"It's Marcella!" Timmy Z panicked.

Craig knew it wasn't, it was something else. "No," he managed to get out, and then he was zapped again. His back arched and contorted back as if he were being electrocuted.

Aisha's dying! went through his head as his body somewhat relaxed.

With his head, Craig motioned to the car. Timmy Z threw Craig's arm over his shoulder and helped him to the car.

•

Marcella was back down in her hidden room trying to locate the Scalici girl once again. The last few times, the eye refused to open all together. Knowing it would weaken her, she took the ritual knife and sliced her palm along the thumb's seam. As her blood began to ooze out, she placed it on the cover. She could feel the book absorbing her blood and life force. Already giving it more blood than was required, she felt the book get even stronger, but hopefully not too strong. When the absorption was done, her hand sealed back up just as it was before.

But why worry? It was her blood that was racing through it.

The eye opened for her. The image was clear as a bell. The Scalici girl was in a kitchen with three other women. Marcella recognized the teenager, but the other two were new.

This isn't right. Over the shoulder on the maid, she saw the clock. It was half an hour ago.

•

Benny had to be careful; Marcella could react violently if she knew he was still watching Timmy Z. Discretion was the key. From his second floor room, he cleaned his gun and listened to Timmy tell his son they were going to get a new tree. Normally, he would have sent someone to follow them. He waited a few minutes, then called the men at the gatehouse. They reported that Timmy and the kid just left in the Mercedes. When he went to call his lookout in town, it dawned on him what was wrong.

•

Marcella was at a loss. She wanted to send a group to get the child, like she did the black bitch. Yet she could not get a location, or even an accurate time line on her. There was magic involved here that was not her own; it could be the only explanation. There was a rap at the cellar door. She knew it was Benny, since he was the only one with balls big enough to come down here.

"This better be good, Benny!" she yelled to him as he walked in.

"Quick question 'ma'am. Do you know where your beloved husband is?" he asked smirking.

"He took Georgy into town to get another tree to plant. One of the maids told me. Now leave him alone," she warned.

"'Ma'am, if you were going to get a tree to plant, would you take a $60,000 sports car?" he asked. "He also told Joey to come back to the house. When he went back to the garage, he found the air had been let out of all the tires. Now I know you said not to..."

"Get him back to me! He'll pay for this for the next thousand years! And..." she stopped cold. Benny saw her shift gears. "He's taking Georgy away! Don't just stand there, get after them!" she commanded more out of fear than anger.

•

Lying down and wedged into the back seat of Timmy Z's car felt like being trapped in a leather upholstered coffin. They made it past the gatehouse without a hitch while each heartbeat brought life back into Craig. His partner was down, he could feel her dying. Since he was with Christina the night before, he just seemed to know a lot of things.

"Okay, don't fade out on me, buddy," Timmy called back to Craig.

"I'm here big guy. Just get to the gas station, I'm parked behind it. Where's the tape?" he finally asked.

"Taped to my leg," he answered.

"What tape, Dad?" Georgy asked.

"Um, a secret tape. If you see mommy again, don't tell her about it," Timmy said patiently, as if explaining the rules of a game.

They got to the old gas station in a minute. The rusted pumps stood like old soldiers still at attention.

Craig popped up out of the seat. "Pull behind, and we'll switch cars. This thing stands out a tad."

Timmy parked and carried Georgy out of the car. "All's going well, don't ya think?"

"The tape please," Craig asked, jumping up out of his casket.

The smile that had been on Tim's face waned a bit, then he dropped his drawers. Strapped to his thigh was the cassette, Craig's salvation.

"Is that evidence, or are you just happy to see me?" Craig laughed.

"Can we get out of here now?" Timmy ripped the cassette off.

"Sure thing. How are ya doin', kid?" Craig asked Georgy as he ruffled his hair.

Georgy smiled and gave him a thumbs up.

•

Benny's Corvette was the first car re-inflated and past the gate. The rest soon followed.

•

It felt good driving his own car again. Craig knew every little nuance about it, how fast to take a turn, when to gun it after a curve in the road. Plus, the fucker was fast. Yet he drove at normal speed back down the road. A speeding hot rod was sure to get attention. In his rearview mirror, he saw the gleam off a Corvette speeding down the road.

"Duck down guys. They're on the road," Craig warned.

Georgy and Timmy slid down onto the floor while Craig slipped on sunglasses. He rolled up his sleeve to give that added punk kid look. It was Christina that said he still looked like a teenager. God, he loved her. While the Corvette drew closer, Craig popped a cigarette in his mouth and acted cool.

"Don't you think you should light that, tough guy?" Timmy asked from under the seat.

"Oops," Craig kidded and popped in the cigarette lighter.

Craig lit his smoke at the same time Benny roared past. He hoped he didn't know his car. Looking over he saw Benny and one of the Dragon's hoods giving him the once-over. Craig nodded and gave him the peace sign. The Corvette raced ahead like the *Starship Enterprise* going into warp drive.

"So far, so good." Craig watched the car disappear over the next hill.

"Are we going right to the airport?" Timmy asked.

"Nope, she'll expect that," Craig replied, accidentally inhaling the cigarette.

"Harm my son and you'll pray for death." Marcella's voice came out of Benny's car stereo.

"Nothing will happen to him. Can you see them?" Benny asked his radio.

"No! It's like when I try to see Scalici. It's blocked," the radio answered.

"That's it!" Benny yelled.

•

Craig crested the hill and saw no traffic. "Looking good, guys."

From behind a roadside billboard, Benny's Corvette pulled out and alongside of them.

"Looking bad, guys," he smiled and gave them the peace sign again.

Both Benny and the others just stared at him. Craig then lowered his one finger, leaving the middle one up and hit the gas. The Mustang's engine jumped as they took off.

"Sit up and buckle yourselves in," Craig cried as they reached speeds over eighty.

The road was straight and could handle high speeds, but it would eventually have a sharp turn. The quick lead Craig had was eroding away and he needed to do something fast. So he slowed down. Benny quickly pulled alongside and the Dragon's man pointed a gun at him. Timmy held Georgy close.

"Pull over!" the hood commanded.

"No." Craig twiddled his fingers at him. "How are you going to stop me without getting Broom-Hilda pissed?"

Craig knew Marcella would mutilate anyone that harmed her son. He floored it again, knowing he had to win the race before the others caught up and outnumbered him. By now he saw several other cars from the mansion come into view. All they had to do was get ahead of him and block the road. The speeds were getting higher again as they twisted around the hills. Thank God no one was out on the road. Like a beacon Craig saw what he wanted to see and drove right past it. When he saw the last car pass it, he went into action.

"Hold on!" he shouted as he slammed on the brakes.

Benny's Corvette veered to the side and flew past. Craig threw the car in reverse and peeled out toward the oncoming cars. One by one they went off the road as he barreled toward them.

"Out of the way you maniacs!" he yelled at them, and then looked to Timmy. "Sunday drivers!"

Timmy gulped. Going backwards, Craig made it to his destination, a narrow dirt road.

"Dad, I don't like this game," Craig heard Georgy say over the engine.

"Almost over kid," Craig said as they reached the meadow.

In the middle of the field was a helicopter. "Messinal Industries" was painted in big bold letters on the side. What really surprised Craig was its pilot—his father in-law.

"What the hell are you doing?" Craig screamed.

"Shut up and get in asshole!" Thor hollered back louder. "My jet is gassed and ready in Jersey.

"You're not supposed be flying this!" Craig argued while Timmy Z. and Georgy climbed in.

"Bull!" Thor yelled.

A slug tore a hole in the chopper's glass. Craig spun around and returned fire on Benny and his sidekick.

"Get out of here!" Craig shouted.

The last thing he wanted to do was leave Craig behind, but he had no choice. He pulled the throttle up and lifted off the ground.

"You can't leave him, they'll kill him!" Timmy screamed, grabbing Thornton's arm.

"If we take a round in the prop, we're not leaving either," Thor replied. "Don't worry, he's lucky"

"Dad, is Benny trying to kill us?" Georgy asked, now trembling.

"Yes, he is," he replied as the chopper flew over the trees to safety.

•

Watching from her book, the helicopter came into focus as soon as it left Craig. "There you are!" she hissed to herself. She tried to will the chopper to land. Too bad for her she had given too much blood to the book. She wasn't strong enough.

"Georgeeeeeeeeeeee!" she cried, slamming her fist on the eye.

•

So here I am, my second gunfight in less then twenty-four hours. "Give it up, Benny! I've got you surrounded!" Craig yelled.

"Fuck off, pig!" Benny answered along with some hollow points, hitting the Mustang.

"Since you lost Timmy and the kid, Marcella is going to roast you alive," he called back, returning fire. "Why don't we grab a pitcher and get shit-faced."

More shells hit the car.

"Hey, I tried," Craig added, then shot Benny's sidekick in the left eye.

"Just you and me now, motherfucker!" Benny shouted, almost sounding happy about the situation.

Craig had to move. At any moment the rest of the gang was going to barrel down the road and fill him with holes. That's what Benny was holding out for. If this were all happening on TV, he'd have a convenient hand grenade to lob.

Humm, and what does a grenade do? It goes boom.

"Hey Benny, you know what makes your Vette a piece of crap right now?"

"Cops can't afford it!" Benny answered.

Craig responded like a game show host: "Bing! Sorry, incorrect. The answer is 'made of fiberglass'."

Benny looked to where the gas tank was on his prized car. He jumped out of the way just as Craig's lead present hit its target. Like a mini-A-bomb, the red Corvette exploded in a fiery mushroom. Exposed, Benny started shooting wildly at Craig.

"Give it up! I have a clear shot!" Craig yelled at him taking aim.

"You'd be doing me a favor!" Benny shouted, walking and firing.

"I don't want to do this!" Craig yelled, feeling increasingly sick to his stomach. "It doesn't make sense."

"What has lately?" Benny replied and fired again, grazing Craig's cheek.

He hated shooting a man standing right in front of him. He aimed for his leg and fired. The slug landed high, right in Benny's gut. He went down with a grunt, hard. He arched his back for a moment then lay motionless. Sudden nausea filled Craig and he puked up pure bile. There was no food in the vomit. His head was spinning and he could hardly get to his driver's seat. He still had to get his ass out of there. The Mustang started up in spite of its new ventilation. He threw it in drive and drove past the burning wreckage for the paved road beyond.

•

The eye remained shut, despite Marcella's pleas. She felt all she had built crumbling around her. It would be hours before her strength came back in full. If she had only held off giving the book more blood, she could have stopped all this. Her husband was able to betray her and kidnapped their son all because she was distracted—distracted by Scalici. Revenge was hers at all cost.

•

Craig made it to the road and backtracked so as not to meet up with the posse that went off the road before. There were other ways of getting back to the highway. Going back there, though, he found the posse waiting for him.

"Damn it!" he screamed and twirled the car around. Racing back the other way, he knew there would be another roadblock waiting. "Oh, what the fuck," he told himself. He'd just ram anything in his way.

Just as he suspected, there was a line of cars blocking the road ahead of him. Pushing the pedal harder, he decided to take as many out as he could. The blockade grew closer at a phenomenal speed. He could now make out the faces of the three in front, Chip, Jerry, and Tanya.

"SH-I-I-I-T!" he wailed as he slammed on the brakes.

He felt the Mustang fishtail and spin out of control. The world spun in a flash, around and around, while he continued to slam the brake pedal with all his bodyweight.

190

"*Stop!*" he screamed, and the car stopped short like a dog obeying a command.

Looking out, he saw a two dozen cops and troopers peering up over their blockade.

"Hi, guys," is all Craig could say.

Chip was on the ground spread-eagled.

"You dick," he mumbled.

The rest of the cars came over the ridge and every loaded gun swung around and pointed directly at them. With a chorus of screeching tires, they slammed on the brakes and headed back the way they came. The cops and troopers jumped in their cars and gave chase. It was only then that Craig noticed his friends were all dressed in plain clothes.

"How did you guys plan this?" Craig asked, stepping out of the car. His knees were still shaking.

"Thank Trent Gold. Most of the cops in the state saw his expose' on you. Basically, it pissed everyone off," Jerry explained.

"Besides, we were all up here on a seminar for police and driver safety," Tanya added.

"I had a feeling this was a good place for one," Chip said. "Especially since we all abandoned you last night."

The pain in Craig's side returned tenfold. "Aisha? Where's Aisha?"

The three looked to the ground.

"They ambushed her," Chip said quietly.

"How is she?" Craig felt nauseous again.

"Not good, buddy." Chip whispered, getting moist in the eyes.

"Get me there please, before I pass out."

Chapter 13

CHRISTINA, AISHA & MARCELLA

Christina read up on all of the dragon and witchcraft information at her disposal. Nothing had shed any light on what was going on. Her dreams had told her she was pregnant, but that's all they did. If she was a witch, she only had the power of second sight. The thought of parenthood was not as consuming as she had thought. Blaming it on denial, she still had a feeling that it wasn't going to happen. Craig's friend, Chip, had called her and said that Craig was fine, but his partner had been shot and was near death.

From her back patio, she watched the day slowly turn to night. It would have been a perfect time for a glass of wine, but that was out of the question. Mineral water did just as nicely. When she thought of everything that had brought her to this point, she could hardly believe it was actually her life she was remembering. Watching her mother drown, her brother shot and bleeding to death before they came here were all unfocused pictures now. They were to be put away, only to be taken out when her child was old enough to see and understand them.

She was going to be a mother.

All the evil in the world seemed to vanish when a baby comes into the world. What forces were working to bring her and Craig to this point? What control did she have on those forces? She desperately wanted to go to the hospital and meet with Craig, but what he had to say to Aisha was personal and private, even more intimate than her own relationship with him. Again she looked to the water, it appeared black as silk with its soft ripples going on for miles.

He might need me there, went through her head. The hospital is less than an hour away...

The decision was made and she went back inside. Out in the bay, the massive head of the dragon rose out of the water.

•

Germaine sat at his wife's side in ICU. A unit of blood marked B+ dripped into Aisha's arm at a steady rate. A large crucifix hung over her bed like an alter. Craig walked in slowly and thanked God that her children were sleeping in the waiting room. For all the years he had known her and her family, he had only met her husband three times. The smells of the room immediately brought him back to when his own father was dying. The blend or urine and antiseptic was a scent you never forget.

"How's she doing?" Craig asked, not knowing what he would say next.

"They almost lost her on the table. They had to shock her with the paddles," Germaine explained as he wiped sweat off of her forehead.

"I'm so sorry. It all my fault," Craig sobbed.

"No, it's was evil's fault, not yours," Germaine Barlow said in a low, radiant voice.

Aisha's eye's fluttered open.

"Honey, it's me. Can you hear me?" Germaine asked.

She opened her lips a bit and barely got out, "Yes."

"Let me get the nurse," he offered, but she reacted harshly.

"No, I want to talk to Craig."

Germaine looked at Craig and started to get up, but she grabbed his hand.

"I didn't tell you to go!" she said as forcefully as she could. Then she fixed her eyes on Craig. "I met someone Craiger. I was your mother."

Fighting back more tears, he went along with her delusion. "Did she say anything?"

"She's sorry that she wasn't around for you. That you must protect your children. They are our hope," she said with an amazing force.

"Relax, you need to rest," Craig whispered, as Germaine washed her head again.

"Is she dead?" she suddenly asked.

Germaine looked at them both like they were plotting a murder.

"No, she's not dead," Craig replied, then smiled, "But she'll be put away for life. The D.A. is listening to the tape now."

Aisha raised her hand, I.V. and all, and pointed to Craig, "No, you must kill her! None of our families are safe unless she's dead!"

"Honey, relax," Germaine pleaded, just coming short of tying her down.

"We're not safe!" she exclaimed, summoning the nurses over. "None of us."

•

Christina drove along the Sunrise Highway heading for Amityville. The road was clear since everyone had reached their Labor Day locations long ago. It was too late for people getting off from work, and too early for the drunks. She kept her right hand over her stomach and thought of what a magical world it was.

A child was growing inside her. A man she actually loved would be happy to see her.

With the radio off, she left the window open and listened to the music of the outdoors blowing past her. The air was the right mix of summer warmth with just a hint of autumn coolness. Her hand started to shake a little on the wheel. Thinking nothing of it, she closed the window of the Triumph for warmth. Her hand started to shake more and the feeling of happiness quickly vanished. Not knowing why, she looked in the rearview mirror and saw the great winged beast in the air behind her. Its wingspan took up more space than the mirror provided. Small jets of flame came out of its nostrils. She looked forward too much to see and almost swerved off the road. Overcorrecting, she nearly flipped the car.

Like Craig had done earlier, she floored the gas. A brilliant flash appeared behind her just as she took off. But it wasn't white like lighting, it was orange like fire.

Not daring to look, she started to think. By the hospital was South Oaks, a private hospital constructed on both sides of the highway. A tunnel connected the two. She raced the car as fast as she could, blowing right through all the red lights. She allowed herself a quick look. She was further away than she thought. The turnoff was coming quick.

Again like Craig, she slammed on the brakes as hard as she could. The Dragon soared right over her with amazing power. The car felt as if it were going to be sucked right along with it. She immediately turned off the lights and pulled into the hospital grounds.

Dozens of trees canopied her car. Almost concealed was the tunnel, she darted her car into it and laid low. The dim orange lights were almost the same color as her car. She hoped it would help. Outside she heard the wind whoosh by like a storm gust. A few limbs cracked as if they were screaming in pain. She could hear them thud on the ground beneath. She knew she had to get out of there, leave the car and run for the hospital.

Thinking that every little sound might be heard, she opened the door ever so slowly and crept out. For an animal the size of a football field, it was very silent. She took off her shoes and ran to the far end of the tunnel. Peering out, the sky was still clear with no sign of a dragon. Before her were the fields of oak trees that gave the place its name.

Christina made a dash for it, hiding in a thicket of bushes under the trees. Behind her she could see a commotion at the other side of the highway. Not wanting to stick her head out, she watched the tunnel. The light inside flickered abnormally, then she heard another whoosh.

This time, though, it was like a giant bellows taking in air. Suddenly, a massive flame roared out of the tunnel. Her car was shot out like a huge cannonball and hurled into the side of one of the buildings.

Now she knew: if she did hide in the hospital, this thing would kill everyone inside. So she froze. Like a scared animal she stayed put. In the parking lot, two scaly legs landed silently. Each one was bigger than any of the trees on the property. Its head lowered to the ground and started to sniff. One by one, the lights in the buildings came on. The dragon immediately turned its head and looked. Christina remained silent and held her stomach tight as the dragon began to move to the hospital.

"No!" came out of her mouth without her realizing it.

The dragon swung its head and neck around like a living crane. It glared at her with its orange eyes.

"Please, no. I'm…" before she could finish, the dragon let loose its fiery wrath upon her.

•

"No!" Craig yelled in the waiting room where he had been sleeping. "Christina!" The explosions had already awakened Chip and the others moments earlier. "Christina!"

He ran into the hallway and down to the window. A half mile away he saw flames shooting up into the sky. Chip came running up behind him.

"Craig, what the hell are you doing?" Chip asked grabbing his shoulder.

"She dead! Oh my God, she's dead. She got her," Craig cried.

"Who got who?" Chip asked, trying to hold him from jumping out the window.

"The dragon. It just killed Christina and our baby!" Craig screamed like a mad man.

"Craig!" Germaine's voice called out. "She wants to talk to you."

•

Aisha was flailing in her bed and pulling at her tubes.

"Get him in here!" she yelled again and again.

Craig ran to her side. "Calm down, partner. You're going to start bleeding again," he said, as they all tried to hold her down.

"Shut the hell up!" she demanded. "Remember what I showed you at the jewelry store?"

"Of course I do," he answered as she looked down into his very soul.

"Then learn from that. Open your eyes, son," she said calmly and smiled. Then she faded away.

In seconds the nurses and doctors were on her with the crash cart. Craig walked away quietly.

"Craig, what's going on?" Chip asked him.

"On the way here, didn't you tell me they found Trent's body?" Craig asked.

"Yeah, up in Connecticut," Chip answered. "The same way they found Gercio."

"It was in a stable, wasn't it?" He asked.

Surprised, Chip agreed. "Yeah, but I didn't tell you that."

"Chip, I need to get to Dune Point right now."

•

Marcella managed to get away from her mansion before it got raided. Weakened from the blood loss, it was hours before she was back to full strength. She knew she'd have to lay low for a while. The book was safely locked in the cellar. Its hidden entrance would never be found. Once her exposure subsided in a couple of years, she'd rebuild. For now, she had a mission. Since Scalici took away her child, it was time for her to do the same. The book may have been hazy, but it showed her right where to go.

Standing among the trees at Dune Point, she willed herself not to be seen. This would be it, she was going to let the detective live, knowing his daughter died a slow agonizing death. Maybe she'd even place a curse on his head to boot. After all, she was the most powerful witch to ever walk the Earth.

Marcella made her way through the trees to the beach house where Meredith was sleeping. The nameplate in front was the same as the one on the side of the helicopter. In the window, she saw the old man that piloted the thing. He was asleep with a glass of what looked like cognac. The little girl was near.

"Mar-cell-a." A woman's voice called to her.

The witch turned around to see no one.

"What's the matter, can't you see me?" the voice taunted.

"Show yourself, witch! I have a bone to pick with you!" Marcella sneered.

"And I with you," the voice replied.

"Do you think you can overpower me?" Marcella cackled.

"Oh yes," the dragon chuckled.

"Then show yourself!" Marcella commanded.

From behind the most minute of trees, the dragon stepped out in her human form. Her eyes glaring orange to let the witch know exactly what she had stepped into.

"You? You're a witch?" Marcella asked in total disbelief.

"Oh no, not a witch. Loved your dad. All that aftershave gave his flesh a sharp tanginess." The dragon laughed, her voice going four octaves lower.

"Oh, no. Satan help me," Marcella cried.

With a voice like Satan himself, the dragon laughed at the witch.

"I curse thee!" Marcella cried. "I curse thee and thy children."

The dragon laughed harder and began morphing into the beast.

Marcella screamed.

Seconds later, Thornton ran outside with his gun in hand. He could have sworn he heard a scream. All he found though was the wind and the night.

•

Two hours later, Craig showed up at the doorstep of the beach house. The police boat had brought him over, and then took both him and Meredith back. Sandra's pleas to spend the night fell on deaf ears, though he did promise to call them in the morning. After profusely thanking Thornton again and again, the police took father and daughter back home.

Chapter 14

THE DRAGON REVEALED

On the boat ride home, Craig questioned all of his priorities. Killing people, even though they were evil, left a bitter taste in his mouth. Taking a boy away from his mother, even though she was evil, also left a bitter taste in his mouth. It was ironic, he thought, that Marcella was the embodiment of evil and still a better mother than Trish.

The old Mustang was still able to drive the two of them back to their home. Meredith slept soundly on his shoulder. At a red light, Craig looked at his daughter and marveled about how beautiful she was. Her skin was so delicate with those big lashes of hers. What a heartbreaker she was going to be. Too bad Aisha and Trish wouldn't be here to see her. If only Sandra and Thornton had been better parents for Trish. Now that they appeared to know better, he had no problem letting them help raise his daughter. Particularly since old Thor risked his life to help a stranger. He sincerely hoped that Timmy Z and Georgy would do well in Israel. He dreaded what he had to do next.

At last Craig pulled into the house he called home. The Chevy was parked where it always was, and he pulled in next to it as he always did. Remnants of chalk marks from the body outline and crime scene were still there despite the obvious cleaning effort. Cradling Meredith in his arms, he carried her to the front door. Enjoying the night air, Mrs. McIlvain sat at her post on the porch.

"Detective, is it safe for you to be here?" she asked with deep concern.

"As safe as I'll ever be," he replied, as Meredith stirred to life.

"Is she still after you?" Mrs. McIlvain asked, looking more and more like a grandmother.

"Oh no, ding dong, she's dead."

"Who's dead, Daddy?" Meredith asked from her fuzzy consciousness.

"The big bad witch, honey."

Meredith rubbed her eyes, then hugged her dad.

"How are you dear?" Grandma McIlvain asked.

"I'm okay now," Meredith smiled. "I'm glad to be home."

"It's good to have you back. I left some cookies for you by your door, why don't you get some?" The old lady smiled.

"In a minute, hon." Craig said to Meredith, "I want to discuss something with Mrs. M and her family. Okay?"

"Oh, they're all asleep. I'm the only insomniac," the old woman said.

"Actually, you're the only one there is. Period," Craig replied.

"What was that, dear?" Mrs. McIlvain asked.

"I hate to admit it, but I'm one lousy detective," Craig announced to both of them.

"No, you're a wonderful detective!" Mrs. McIlvain insisted.

"In all my years here, I have yet to ever see two of you together. I heard your voices arguing. I've even seen one go in a door and another come out. Yet never did I ever see any of your family together."

"That's not your fault, dear. This is your home, you shouldn't have to think and be paranoid," she said, then morphed into Mrs. Snow. "I'm glad you came back."

"Where was I to go? It's not as if I could hide from you," he said, as Meredith just watched. "Why did you do it?"

"They were out to harm you and the family we built here. After that son of a bitch threatened you on TV, I couldn't let him live," she said in Mrs. Snow style. "What finally tipped you off about me?"

"Cranberry Farms. Only Meredith and I were there, but it was you she cried to when we got back. I'm glad you didn't kill any of them," Craig said. "But you didn't have to kill the others."

"Of course I did, they wanted to break up the family." She morphed into Jeannine. "I'd do anything to keep us together. If you'd only told me who was after you, all this would have been avoided."

"Thornton finally told you after he got home. They told me you were there," Craig said, as Jeannine got up to pinch Meredith's nose.

"You still love me, kid?" Jeannine asked.

Meredith nodded her head.

"She killed your mother, Meredith." Craig said. "If Grandma and Grandpa tried to take you, they would have died, too."

"They really turned out to be nice people. I'm glad I didn't kill them," Jeannine confessed, causing Meredith to recoil a bit. "Don't be frightened, we'll be together forever now. No one can separate us."

Craig's anger started to show in a very controlled manner. "You murdered Christina! Were you *that* jealous?"

"She was a witch, but nowhere near as powerful as Marcella," she said, getting defensive.

"You lie, you couldn't stand me being happy with another woman. It could only be you," he snapped at her crossly.

"And why not! I'm perfect for you! I'm everything you never had growing up, Grandmother, mother, wife!" she fired back, becoming cross herself.

"Are you going to marry Jeannine, Daddy?" Meredith asked.

"No! She's a murderer, and she killed my baby," Craig said to both Meredith and Jeannine.

"What are you talking about? I would never have harmed a child! Even Marcella's!" she exploded.

"Christina was pregnant. The two of us knew from the moment of conception," Craig seethed.

Jeannine gasped, "Oh, no. Tell me you're lying."

Craig just stared at her.

"Oh, no, I didn't mean to!" she cried, falling to her knees. "If I had only known." She looked up to him with her big blue eyes soaked in tears. "But there's always *our* children?"

Craig laughed. "You're really delusional, dragon lady."

Jeannine crossed her brow. "No Craig, we *will* have children. They're already conceived." She stood up and held his stiff body.

"What are you talking about? Dragon's can only mate with other dragons and witches. I am not a witch," he said, shaking his head.

"You're correct. You're not a good detective, and you're not a witch. You're a warlock," she said, getting the upper hand.

Craig put Meredith down and looked into Jeannine's eyes. He knew she wasn't lying.

"That amazing luck of yours. You think that was by chance? You have been manipulating things your whole life, Craig. You've made this perfect world for yourself. The other night we conceived six children. I laid the eggs early this morning." Jeannine leaned forward and softly kissed him on the lips.

"Does that make *me* a witch?" Meredith asked.

"Yes." Jeannine bent down to her. "And a very powerful one, too. That's why Marcella could never find you with a spell, or your dad. And as you get older, your powers will grow."

"No, this isn't possible," Craig whispered, feeling his feet begin to sway.

"You and Christina weren't *meant* to be together, you just sensed each other. That's how your kind reproduces. I bet the main reason Marcella hated you so was that she was also attracted to you."

"This is a nightmare," he said, sitting down in Mrs. McIlvain's chair. Meredith came over and stood by his side.

Jeannine started to cry again. "I promise you, if I had known she was expecting, I never would have harmed her."

"You lie!" he yelled. "It would have made you want to kill her even more. You may be a dragon, but you're a jealous woman even more!"

"No! I love you! I love Meredith!" she sobbed, grabbing his hand.

"Murderer!" he yelled, shoving her away onto the ground.

"Do you know how long I have known you? I sensed your power from the day you were born. Your mother's craft was very strong, and shined like a beacon. I cried when she died. I was there your whole life." She morphed into a familiar woman he couldn't quite remember.

"I was the school nurse at your grammar school." She morphed again into his next door neighbor as he grew up in Brooklyn. "I was also Miss Webber. Remember?"

"No. It can't be," he muttered.

Meredith came to his side.

She morphed back to Jeannine. "Shall I continue?"

"No!"

"I felt bad for you. Helped raised you. Then I fell in love with you. I knew your marriage wouldn't have worked. Otherwise I would have stopped it." She looked to Meredith. "Well, maybe not."

"But you kill people," Craig said.

"And you don't?" she retorted, standing up.

"That was self-defense! I had no choice!"

"Do you realize you killed your father? You willed him to death." she revealed.

"No!"

"He was a miserable bastard."

"If you knew this about me, why didn't you let me know?"

"Because you were so innocent. You have a good heart. You would never willingly harm anyone unless they deserved it. That's why I love you so much."

"Impossible! This is all nonsense."

"There's more to this planet than the world you made for yourself. But you chose to look away. So, I'm so evil. Look at yourself, we all have evil within us. Just give us power, and you can see that we usually act upon it."

"But I could have saved Aisha. Hell, I could have stopped several wars," Craig muttered in a haze.

"And that would have caused all the more evil. People must choose their actions," Jeannine explained. "Now why don't we become a family again? We have six on the way."

"How long before they are born, um...hatched?" Craig asked.

"About a year and a half." She sat down on his lap and put her arms around him.

"Will they age slower than the rest of us?"

"Yes, but you age slower, too. Why do you think you look so young? And you're such a wonderful father," she added, putting her head in his chest.

Craig looked at her and then his daughter.

"No," he said with a note of finality.

Filled with confusion, Jeannine looked at him with those blue eyes again.

"You said it yourself. I'm oblivious to the outside world. How could I possibly raise more children if I'm one myself?" He sighed, "I know you can force me to be with you. But the simple fact is, I do not love you. Children shouldn't be raised in a home without love. I choose not to be with you."

Jeannine slapped him across the face. "You're going to abandon your children?"

"If I didn't know for a certainty that you were capable of raising them on your own, then of course not. I will find them when I can be of some help to them."

She slid off his lap and looked to the two of them.

"You can always force me," he said.

"So that's how it's going to be? No, I won't force you." She looked to Meredith and scooped her in her arms for a prolonged hug. "I'll always be there for you kid." She put the girl down.

"One thing more," Craig added. "I didn't know I killed my father. You knew you were killing Christina and Trish."

"Choices, Craig. The reasons we make them will always be a mystery."

And with that, she disappeared into the night behind her. All they heard was a gust of wind and silence.

"Was she bad, Daddy?" Meredith asked, sitting in Craig's lap just like Jeannine had just done moments before.

"It's complicated, honey," he said, kissing her on the top of her head.

"What are you going to do now?" she asked, cuddling up in his arms.

"Go back to school, I guess," he answered.

"I'm glad we're home," she whispered.

"So am I, dear. So am I."

Printed in the United States
120825LV00002B/73/A